Short stories

Popular fairy tales: Children of the train

Don't make some folktales around the world out of funny extra oddities, including this government of the people deployed in Australia, Europe, America and started talking about my Australian little attention trails due to the fact that there are more kids than usual, so that the share of the States is several times the fabric in any city or town again, in fact, the country was overflowing with crazy children. wherever you go, you will find children playing, or chosen ones, or studying, etc. This is a surprise for researchers and children in Australia, so I started some research in this country to see the mystery grow.

The researchers studied everything in the country, water, air, plants and food that the population eats, but did not find any difference from the rest of the cities and towns .. they examined the bodies of men for sure and did not find anything extraordinary, finally they examined the gene and did not find any difference from the genes of other Australians .. what is the secret, if there are explosives in fertility? Nobody knows, and in the end, after I killed the explorers who were desperate to find out the secret, they left the city and left ..

But the city authorities, in a last attempt, sent one of the best police investigators, already with a bug, to reveal the secret ..

The detective went to the city and began to carefully check all the corners and the Ark, observing both the small and the large in the actions of the population, but finding nothing unusual ..

On the last night at the dacha, the detective worked until late in the evening, making his return to the hotel in the big city, adjacent to the dacha for the woman hard, so he decided to stay at the dacha in the guest house of one of the houses ..

The group slept comfortably that night, in the silence and noise of the big city, but the decisions of the former fifth dawn woke up, the detective rolled in his voice like a thunderclap, not a single corner of the room was shaken in his power ... in fact, the sound was similar to the whistle of a freight train that cuts through the country every day at five o'clock in the morning ... and of course that voice was enough to wake up most, if not all of the population ..

The next day he packed his luggage and returned to the capital, and immediately upon his return called the boss to look at the result of his investigation, the detective looked at the boss with a malicious smile on his lips, and then said calmly and confidently:

- Of course, I solved the riddle! ... It's just that there is a freight train crossing the country every day at five o'clock, the train is called a whistle when it passes the city, which leads to a stop of most of the population, and from that time it is too early to get out of bed, and at the same time, too late to go to bed again sleep .. the population was awake in their beds and spending time in something entertaining was couples having sex! ... And this is already the reason for increased pregnancy and childbirth in the rest of the cities and villages of the country, they have sex almost every day! "

President of a company called vagia mouth, does it make sense .. the reason for the increase in fertility is the train whistle ..

The president had to submit a report to his boss, whom they instructed in the course to change the trajectory of the train in order to pass through the city at five in the morning, and only one year pass until the birth rate in the country returns, the nature of the case is the same as in all other cities

George Steney is the youngest ever sentenced to death in US history .

George six is the youngest person sentenced to death in United States history, the electric chair is too big for him, I owe it in a few minutes, and that was 1944.

George was only six years old at fourteen, which even today is considered the youngest death row in modern United States history.

After six years, mystery and controversy still surround the village on all sides, and the trial is short-lived, everything happened in its simplicity, alarming. I owe George a black boy for the double murder of two white girls, the first of whom was named Betty June

(Petit Yun). You and Mary Emma Thames (Mariam Ama Eltaimes) are 8 years old, on the county calendar - South Carolina.

On March 23, 1944, the bodies of two girls were found, missing within 24 hours, and they were beaten to death .. but the question arises, what elements bind the boy in this case? ...

And the answer ... nothing but his own testimony that the death boxes claimed due to specialization in the investigation of such issues then, interestingly, he went to tell the research group, said:

"I saw two girls lying on the ground, and one of them is still alive ..." - and then paused and continued to speak, saying that these two girls passed me and they were using two bicycles, and I asked them where I can find several kinds of flowers.
After the body was found, little George was arrested on charges of first-degree murder, the boy is the only suspect and has not called any other witnesses to testify. After ten minutes of discussion, the jury, which included all members of the Chamber, sentenced him to death in the electric chair.

The government is unfair to the right of George stirring to protest against large unions, religious organizations naacp, an organization that defends the civil rights of brown-skinned citizens.

Three months have passed since the crime was committed, there was not a single new case on the morning of June 16, 1944 in Colombo prison, the boy was walking to the death cell, he holds a copy of the Bible in his hand. And he found that the executioner finds it difficult to associate George because of his small size, the appearance of his meta-analysis of the heart with the severity of pain.

After four minutes of sharp pain, the death of my sixth George was announced.

His case lasted more than half a century, controversial until 2005, when three lawyers reopened the case and after extensive research declared the innocence of the hammer boy! ... But his criminal record has not been reopened by American justice. Became the symbol of George the Sixth.

You knew the United Nations grew up in a brothel!

Prostitution is the oldest profession in history, I think prostitutes first appeared in the days of the cave, perhaps I traded in services with a piece of meat from a prey caught by one of the men. Since then, I knew that the problem I was looking for did not open up, it almost creates a century or a country of prostitutes, most of them work secretly because of society's perception of the inferiority of their functions, but they also received wide recognition, and even this one became an empress! ... Believe it or not, dear reader, the Byzantine Theodora was a prostitute and a stripper, on the streets of Constantinople - Istanbul - in front of the throne of the empire in the seventh century, but this is another story that has not replaced them now.

States control supplies, like any profession, erring who think that casual prostitution does not obey the system, you can believe that some street prostitutes, whores, brothels speak to the system precisely and strictly. The street prostitute ate right and beat, neglected and even killed, the whore from the open brothel kept the concern of providing part of her wages to a pimp or pimp who spoke shelter and protection to bring clients. This is a sign of a parasite that has evolved over time into a major industry generating billions of dollars a year and giving birth to months of pimps throughout history, including the lady we'll be talking about today, Sally Stanford, who ran one of America's finest and most sophisticated brothels. , worked when some of the most beautiful, cute and intelligent girls were the most stylish in the world. It is not surprising then that crowds of celebrities from all sides flock to the brothel, or rather to the palace of their sheikh, which is located on one of the prestigious avenues of the city of San Francisco.

The list of visitors included politicians, government officials, high-ranking artists, as well as Poles of industry and commerce, army and police officers, ambassadors, foreign ministers and even princes and kings, every evening there was an evening of the noisy best Magna, dancing and ancient vocals, so that some of the visitors brought their wives with them. That is, the evening always ends in the bedroom with a lot of RDM throughout the building.

Mrs Stanford had her own customer service too, some celebrities said, Come see for yourself, so it was Mrs Stanford who sent her girls to the rooms and suites that kept her secret in upscale hotels away from prying eyes and prying eyes.

Sometimes it was Mrs. Stanford who provided her girls for free, which is what most pimps around the world do to lure government officials and police officers, as well as security guards, into turning a blind eye to what is happening inside a brothel, whose prostitution is illegal in most countries of the world.
Mr. Stanford's merits were not limited only to America, but also to international affairs and the security of the whole world! ... In 1945, a great event took place in the city of San Francisco, the meeting of representatives of fifty countries and one company in negotiations led to the creation of the United Nations as we know it today. But what we don't know, many do not know, is that most of these negotiations were "tough" at Sally Stanford's brothel.

Cana's coat of arms was written about, saying: "The United Nations originated in Sally Stanford's brothel, many of the negotiators were paying clients." According to this one of the clients, these important ones they held many of their meetings in the living room, brothel, these meetings eventually led to the birth of the United Nations.

Sally Stanford herself wrote the following in her diary:

"In the spring of 1945, the United Nations negotiated in large numbers in San Francisco. It was the role of the adult hospitality community in a frantic race with some to win the largest share of the sauce, spices, foreign inspired by these imports. It was fun, let me tell you you!.

When Sergeant Dyer raided the brothel during their stay with me, you claim that diplomatic immunity, I was the one who caught him, held him hostage or prisoner of war or something. Foreign diplomats are left with a lot of what we offer, including sports bedding. Not only because some of them took longer to dip their wick feathers in our bed, that he spent in understanding the United Nations issue, so that some of them never left my house throughout the entire negotiation! ...

Because these boys were very important to the Ministry of Foreign Affairs, so we worked hard to lengthen the time to keep international relations better. "
Oh, irony, the greatest international institution went from brothel to brothel. They negotiate for the security of the world and they have sex, I could say she was a tough negotiator and ferocious, and in my opinion the best proof of the health burden is the idea that politics and religion are two sides of the same medals. With the assertion that a bitch can be watched by politicians, they don't only need you on their bodies, and the depravity of politicians can affect the bodies and minds and pockets of others.

Of course, this does not apply to all politicians, there are honest politicians, inevitably, but they said Unfortunately. Perhaps Sally Stanford, she wanted to reveal herself to the true face of corrupt politics he was suddenly a 1967 conference, a political rally, including the participation of some of the highest people in politics and religion, such as Edward Kennedy, the younger brother of former US President John F. Kennedy. Mrs Stanford challenged on Friday, then I think the listener and I grabbed the microphone, looked for a moment at the faces who are taking to see it, and then went non-stop to get their clients' names in the audience, reach out to them and avoid them. one by one, as if they were carrying a machine gun, and in just a few minutes, turn the party upside down, and she screams from everywhere. The scandal was loud, it turned out that most of those present were Sally Stanford's clients, even those who shook people's heads happened to them for honesty and honor.

Favorite pimp!

Sally Stanford was born in 1903, in the town of Airlie, County of San Bernardino, her real name is Mabel Janice receive an aspirin. Her mother was a teacher. Her father died a little, so she had to leave her studies and help her family - three brothers and one sister. At the age of seven he worked as an accompanist for golfers, billiard balls and rackets. At the age of sixteen, she met a man who let her think he liked her move to help him draft a stolen set of checks, after which he was arrested and imprisoned for two years.

In prison, I became a smuggler, I mean alcohol smuggling, having a thriving career during the period when alcohol was banned in the United States. And through smuggling, collecting good money from Sally, she invested it in the purchase of a small hotel in San Francisco in 1924, and from there she began her career as a pimp and was herself a young man in twenty-fourth. He did not ask for time, even their new craft blossomed and blossomed, so that my Stanford was different from other pimps and pimps not only in that she was smart, playful and gentle, but also in that she chose girls, and our passion for elegance and the amenities were different from other brothels.

Sally was not a beautiful woman, but she was a witch, so I did not execute the lovers who circled around her. Married five times, but did not succeed, and two children, a boy and a girl, he said later, when he grew up, his mother, the pimp Sally Stanford, she was a wonderful mother, very gentle and future for their children, you provide them with the best and most prestigious schools, and everything in her power to stay away from everything that concerns their work.

Sally retired in the fifties. Having opened a restaurant in the heart of Sausalito, California has focused on equality and civil rights issues. People loved the city so much that in 1972 they even elected it mayor.

Sally Stanford died in 1983, about seventy-eight years old.

If it happened, dear reader, that I visited the town of Sausalito in America that day, there would be a fountain for drinking water, built by the inhabitants of the city in honor and in memory of their mayor "pimp" and spoiled Leland.

Omira Sanchez ... the girl who made the world cry

Colombia, a poor and troubled country in northern Latin America, has a volcano called Nevado del Ruiz, perched atop the towering Mount Transfiguration at the foot of the snow-capped mountains around the world. The volcano had been dormant for hundreds of years, but on the night of November 13, 1985, I woke up that sleeping dragon, which suddenly from behind was spewing fire and ash in all directions.

Molten lava flowed from the ash crater towards the slopes in the snow, and the heat melted the snow and floods receded to Seoul at a speed of 6 meters per second to tamp the city air, and small towns scattered down the valley down the mountain.

Flash floods hit the residents while they slept, I took everything in my path .. buildings, cars and people, and then tip some money in the morning it left behind massive destruction and thirty thousand dead.

Even worse for the residents of the affected valley, they live in a remote area surrounded by mountains, making it difficult for them to access aid and assistance, and also waging open war between insurgents, leftists and the Colombian government. That is why the

world has never heard the explosion of a volcano and the tragedy of the population just a few days after the disaster; humanitarian aid and media coverage of this event never matched the scale of the destruction and the large number of victims.
Omayra Sanchez was a beautiful eighteen-year-old girl living with her family in the suburb of Armaguerrero. Her mother was traveling the night the volcano exploded, it was her, her father, her aunt and her little brother. in the house, when I got into the liquidity of the region, the water fast and extreme speed was what threatened their home and neighboring houses.

Thousands of people were buried under the rubble, most of them died on the spot, but some survived, and they spent several hours heavily trapped under the ruins of their homes. Only a few of them were saved, the rest died of suffocation or thirst, it was a bitter agony that had no end but death, and the misfortune of Omer Sanchez was one of those who got stuck, covered in debris to the waist, leading her into the future, covered with water mucus first up to the neck so as not to see the mermaid swimming in a puddle of mud. And on this path, the unfortunate girl remained tied for three days.

He can live, o'mira. if some relatively modern means of escape were provided, or if professional medical personnel were provided, the harsh difficulty of the area that exploded the volcano led to the belated arrival of supplies.

Some rescuers and local residents tried to dig up the girl, dragging her away from the cold, but they were stopped for two reasons: First, because whenever they tried to pull her out, the higher the water drowned her, and secondly, because they found that her legs were stuck under a huge column of concrete, not reformatted, perhaps only with her legs, but the doctors advised not to do this, because the girl was exhausted and would not move by such a *process, since it was impossible to perform this operation with that piece of muddy water, which covers it.*

Rescuers also requested a pump to pump out the water, but the pump never arrived. In the end, however, everyone fell, they realized that they would save the girl's future, and the o'mirs remained poor, locked in this dirty pond, seeing how people die sadly in front of their eyes and it is not from their hands to do something for her. All he can do is toss it into the water from time to time and also talk to her to calm her down and relieve them. The girl herself was brave, despite her pain, she exchanged conversations with people and rescuers, they even sang once about the factor and the salvation of a German, and from time to time asked for milk and soda water, but sometimes she felt that fear begins to cry and pray, this everyone around her was crying and praying for her ... there was nothing more they could do.

He did not work for O'mera's family. only her younger brother, who emerged from the rubble, miraculously did not become infected, only slightly, since her father had already died and was left lying dead under the rubble, as well as her aunt, who sat her body right under my feet, o'mir point stumbling blocks.

On the afternoon of November 16, French journalist Franck Fournier, a reporter from the French journalist, arrived on the outskirts of the city of Omer after a long and difficult journey, the situation was terrible, few rescuers were waiting here and there, the screams of people trapped in the rubble jumped from time to time, desperately seeking help and consolation, but it was impossible to save all this huge number of victims due to lack of support and weak supply capacity.

While Frank wandered around the city center, destroying houses and neighborhoods in search of a touching picture to show it to the world, one of the peasants approached him and said that a girl was stuck there, in need of help. The farmer took Frank to O'mere's pool, he stayed there for almost three days, was exhausted, exhausted and so sick, his eyes were red and bloodshot, his face tensed ... the poor thing finally realized that she could not be saved, and that death was approaching him with a brisk pace, and asked the people gathered around to go and see.

Frank takes a photo of the girl before her death for three hours, he stays with her, watches her and tries to continue her. While the near death by O'mera finally began to hallucinate, I asked Frank to drive her to school so that she would not be constantly late, and told him that she was very worried because she had a math exam and to win it. Then I began to gradually lose consciousness, and before she died, a few minutes later, she opened her eyes and told one of the designers about it, as you want to say in a few words, the girl called on God to save her family, she thanked everyone around them for staying with her through her ordeal ... it was over, and I closed her eyes again, this time forever.

A few days after her death, a photo of her was published in a newspaper in which Frank and quickly circulated these photos and videos in all media .. people felt at peace with the sadness of the girl, many of them freely wondered why they didn't save her? ... Does it make sense to stay alive for three days and not be saved? .- How could you let her die like that ?!

O'mira's image has significantly contributed to raising awareness of the shared need for unity in times of disaster and polisher, as well as the importance of providing urgent relief to disaster-stricken countries, especially the poor, which is why O'mira Sanchez speaks to the camera with her deep red eyes which have become a symbol of international relief operations.

A pure woman left the house of a prostitute

Her story about the Queen filled the confidant of both the Lower East and the West, the first frivolously and awkwardly from the

West, which had no borders and no red lines! ... And at the second stage, both dedication, and they themselves, and their charitable activities are supported by their people.

And it's amazing that both kings lived under the same roof, despite the fact that the former was in contrast to the other! .. Two different variations of the Earth and the sky, and different people and money! ...
Since then, Hyuk had to iron his nails, disobediently disobey customs and traditions, strike at the values and principles of displaying the wall! ... It was a blatant example of female flirting, those women who wait to explode their femininity and their charms before being allowed to associate! I am not restrained by anything and do not stand in the face of the lust for power and any authority! ... He rebelled against her marriage to the sultan "Ahmad Fuad" until she ran away to keep her decision only to her family, they forced her to marry him, he was twenty years older than her, fucked her very hard, and forced her not to disclose his face in front of strangers and was often afraid of his compulsion, and sometimes he locked her inside the walls of the palace and deprived her of seeing his children and was a living servant of not his mistresses to humiliate her and break the ego of the woman inside her! ...

Heck is obtained from them in a strange way, why leave one of the officers or only noble people, and start a relationship with a sinner in order to earn the authority of the Sultan and show him in the form of a stupid husband! ..

And you can imagine, dear reader, if such a woman dies for her husband and becomes free and liberated, then there is no restraining factor and no Zag, no, an unbridled horse will lift from the bowl all the fun up the harem and will not wear it! ... Filled the past with men all over Egypt, until the reserve officers got their share in her boudoir! Until I met the head of the royal court,

*"Ahmed Hassanein Pasha" and was not married, but there was no
such reason to say in the face of the queen's wishes lived as her
slave and lust for her! ... She knew that she loved him at every
opportunity, and was not ashamed of it! He even bowed to Pasha in
the end and married her according to custom, some say secretly,
without the knowledge of King Farouk's son, while others confirm
their knowledge and the fact that Pasha asks the very car to drive
him! ..*

*She changed him to another blindly, even when she found out
about his connection with the airport management, see ordered to
issue a royal order from Egypt, and filled the newspapers then with
news about the conflict between women between Heck and maybe
even the last, when the Heck said: "I am not a singer from simple ..
I'm a princess, "and some doubts about the murder may apply to us
going down and her son, where she fell on the cart that was used
by Sun in the canal while driving her head and running by the driver
and did not find him on impact! ...*

*And when I found out about the relationship with the artist "Mimi
Chakib", I asked the manager of the branch where you work to ask
her what influenced the artist's departure, knowing that they could
not afford benz hake.*

*There was even a case of killing Sparrow in a car accident at the
hands of a drunk English driver on the Qasr el Nil.*

*And the sparrow brought the queen back to her old habits, where
the bacchantes and the lovers who take advantage of them more
than replace her clothes! As a result, their relationship with the king
"Farouk" deteriorated, and the condition of her kidneys forced her
to leave to do whatever he pleased! ...*

*It was her photographs and their relationship that fill the American
and European with the health, regardless of the status of her son
and not her age, who was in the aging stage, and not the office of
the old country she came from, it did not matter to her, only to*

satisfy her own desires so that she was also, which is not her bottom! ...

Even the fact that in the hotel she and her daughter Princess Fathia the relationship of a sinner with a simple employee of the consulate is supported by Riad Gali, and when she wanted to marry him to a Princess, Farouk refused, because he was of a different religion, but the hake insisted on the marriage and when he learned of this from Farouk, he became enraged and issued a royal decree stripping the Queen Mother and Princess of the privilege of their acts of ownership and sources of funds within Egypt.
The staircase of Nazilli and Fethiye, the real money they had left, who lost it all in unsuccessful projects, there were disagreements between Fethiye and her husband, who fired the last five bullets and died, and then tried to commit suicide, but he was rescued at the last moment and brought to justice , sentenced to fifteen years paralyzed and blind, because he was shot in the head during his suicide attempt.
Heck lived alone in an area populated by the poor after breathing between rehab royal palaces! .. and this is a natural finish for only bed games not progressing in her life! I have not succeeded in anything more than working in finance and fondling and teasing each of the mentioned books on the back, even delivering and fulfilling their wishes, refusing the white flag on her body, these were not the ways of her debauchery that move in front of her stones of gold and crumbs, not to mention resisting her spell.
Our article today is not an article historically, as what is human describes the feeling the Queen eventually has for a woman, how other women think of her pain as he leaves his beloved husband to spend his nights in the arms of others. ! ...

Some women produce and visualize and go through it for the dignity of their wounded, while others become hope for the cross or bow to the orders and whine in their hearts that I am going to Dennis Love holding hands with this lover.

And the only "unique" wife of King "Farouk" of the second type, and how not to be, and he is the first man who knocks at the door of her heart and answers them without any resistance from their side? And this is the first hand that touches her, and the first heart surrounds her heart and needs.
The Queen loved her people and her people and worked for them, married them.

Named after the unique because they are unique and unlike him, was the address for the softness and femininity of the Quiet, romantic-loving, hating everything that is noisy. Her real name "Safinaz Zulfikar" is as unique as the name you chose not to King "Farouk" after what he did to his father Sultan " Ahmad Fuad", who met on one of his trips from the mine to Italy. told him that the character is happy and good, and the spell of his magic is the letter "F".
Omar was unique fifteen years ago when I first met Farouk and it was in the palace garden, she saw him standing and the girls crowded around him and they were an offering to him, but Fred had to do the same as she did. and her upbringing prevents her, that it was only that I went and sat down next to her mother, and when he noticed Farouk, she is the only girl who did not stop him, he approached her, greeted her and got to know them.

After several days of receiving a royal invitation by the Zulfiqar family from the Heck queen mother inviting them to accompany the royal family on their winter trip to Europe, and perhaps the days spent on this trip are the happiest days of her life, as she said ...

Farouk was constant stress and inconsistency towards her, treated her differently, feared her cruelly even when she fell once while skiing on the ice, rushed to her and carried her in his arms, and reached out to the violence of his sisters -the princess over her! ...

On this trip, I realized Farouk that this girl is the girl of his dreams, that I always imagine her in awakening and areas, and it is no coincidence that you can leave Egypt on the throne next to him? After my return, I was surprised to the family Zulfiqar bored, facing a student marriage is unique, and only after that did not reach beyond the clouds, and despite his young age and before the insistence of a lover, I bowed to her father and the ceremonies conducted in all parts of the unguarded, saw demobilization in the capital, to watch the procession of the king and his beautiful wife, beloved and that belonged to a family famous in his soul, in the National, decorated streets with lights that are sent on the night of her day in exquisite scenery, the bride was dressed in a dress made especially for her in Paris with long sleeves is built on the wish of Farouk, who was very jealous on them.

After the completion of the ceremony, the newlyweds went to the palace, where peace and quiet reigned. it should be noted that the signing of the charter of the League of Arab States took place in this palace.

It was unique to say: (since my marriage, I have loved hair and you always live with your dreams and feel their pain).
After his return, Farouk chose not to leave his mother and sisters, but to live together in one palace, and this decision had the misfortune of becoming the only one! What was the personality of Bossy like a hake, which left unique and will! To act in the role of "Mary Penitent" in the film (the son-in-law has beautiful women) is the best way and so that all the torment ends! Her life is a living hell, especially when she gave birth to three princesses and did not become the heir to the crown prince.

It was a hake who often said to him: (I brought Fuad the crown, did not see his nation as my officer of the crown)! And this is how the poor thing owns a magic bullet, a male is born to hit her!

Transformed the walls of the palace into wands, locked inside her unique and her dreams! Even Farouk, who was granted patience by his presence next to her, took the worst page from his mother! Indulge in his pleasures and follow his desires, and how the decay genes have already moved on to this! And this began to strain the relationship between Farouk and Unic, as well as the beginning of the collapse and fall of the throne of the uppermost family! ...

She was the wife of the father of the princess "Shvikar", trying to push him into a life of entertainment and the burden of having a batch of corruption that brings girls dressed but naked of all nationalities! And what is Ali Farouk, just to step into the garden to blossom, to taste her nectar! Forgetting your beautiful wife, three princesses and the Motherland, groaning under the shackles of the occupation! ...
And it was often considered unique in leaving him, but each time he had to repent for this life, referring to the fact that he was doing this to save himself from the indignation of the people and said: (I know that these will not be kings, not the king of England and not king of cards). It was a unique opportunity to take pity on you and believe it, but the next morning forget your vows and your promises, and not just remember Guam and its whores! ...

This news became a sign of his women right up to the unique ones in the Palace, especially his relationship with people of art! The relationship between people of the world and people of art, an endless eternal sign !.
It was his relationship with the artist that was full of months of treatment of his women and he spent her nights dissolutely in the Abdin palace, instead of managing the affairs of the government, managing the affairs of his desires and whims! Often he took her with him on trips abroad on his yacht "El Mahrusa", the same yacht that took him out of Egypt after his removal from power! ...

He even bought her a villa so that there would be a place for them away from the eyes of spies, and from there he assures that the king's entry into a full-fledged life was not accidental, the layout of the Mossad was also established, so be close to the people of the palace and places of decision-making, especially in period of the Palestinian war, as it was, it was full to learn the smallest details and to the ear of their decisions, before they officially announce what it cost the king of Egypt and many others! There are claims that what happened to her after that was just revenge on them for the fact that she accidentally died on a mysterious plane. and it's amazing that he was not among the passengers, so I think that one of their stallions has been replaced by the even stranger one that this journalist-passenger "Anis Mansur" who never found his body and found a pair of her shoes! ...

Even the wife of his doctor, Nahed Rashad, did not crawl out of the window of his love! This did not have a strong impact on the political life of Egypt at the time, which led her to think that she was around the corner of Freddie's cropped crown, especially after Farouk singled out a suite next to his wing and appointed her as his sister's maid, Princess FSIS, after the divorce. the last shah of Iran, "Mohammad Reza Pahlavi", and says that the king did not know the nude pictures of the natural world on one of the walls of his palaces! ...

All those ties on the side and "Lily Bought" on the other side! .. This is the same girl who met the king to meet him at the palace to spend the night in natural colors, but he forgot his stuff and went to an urgent meeting (betop file)! Controlled herself by the unique entrance to the apartment and the threat to the safety of her adopted daughter by the magnificent recognition of the library with the signing of her relationship with the sinful bored one and that she often met him in her apartment while the Queen slept at her funeral! Not only was the woman broken and injured inside the unique it, but she insisted on giving the attorney general virtually the full spectrum, and it was a scandal of the highest caliber! ...

Farouk's anger is the rage of a unique gas charge from the point of view, especially after he went out people turned to him with their women, saying: (where is the food, clothes, King of Women?), And did not write him, but calibrated his actions to their mother outside, saying: (Hey Farouk, fuse. Here's your mother from America) and (doesn't tell his mother not to rule the nation).

We can mention the signs of the Farouk case, not to mention the architect of these relations, the secretary of the Italian "Antoine Poli", who was assigned the main role of the pimp, everything is well deserved! His job is to bring girls to the king of mattresses! Sometimes he took ownership of the Golf Drive to select prey on his own, thus stubbornly staying true to his job! ...

Was Farouk leaves unique every night to see a lawyer on the chest of every whore, offering herself on the altar of the war-wish-war of the world, for those who are interested! ...

Before these acts of gross misconduct, Farouk must stand, even a fig leaf in front of him, to cover his nakedness! He fell from the height of the throne of her heart to score well, except for debauchery and vice.! ... The student, in her freedom and dignity, stolen before her insistence, did not find inevitable respect from Farouk, her desires were officially divorced in 1948, despite this divorce, however, the Love Association collected hearts, they were never interrupted one day, he gave her a palace for life, which houses the princess of the little reputation of the palace of the pure, the day she left all the communities that people call

(Came out clean from the house of the bitch) and (out of the house of the underworld by virtue).

In Farouk's attempt to calm down the Egyptian street that inspired that single shot to betray him with one of the princes! But who would believe this shit? The only bright spot and culture in this king's life was unique in that, despite what he did to her, she did

not marry after the decoder whenever one of her fans said:
(marrying Farouk cannot marry after).
Recently, the writer "Lotus Abdel Kareem", who accompanied the
queen in the last five years of her life, that the queen returned to
the king in exile under a contract with a legal official, did not know
them, but is the princess of the large "free download", but the only
one scared him out of fear for her stay in Egypt men of the
revolution! ... So I heard how all the spectators lamented Rome as
more suitable for them at Farouk's funeral, but they went after he
mastered the development of transferring the remains of his
beloved husband to the royal cemetery in the al-Rifai mosque down
at the behest of Farouk before his death, he used respect and
appreciation from everyone and it was a cataract or other rejection
of the request for home hair unique.

I did it for a man who squandered her dignity next to her femininity,
was challenged at the best that women have! But what will she do,
and the Southern Christians have no choice! ...
Do you believe, dear reader, that a noble queen, like a deceased
queen, has nothing poor? Even the palace he received from Farouk
and the state! The picture was headed, and then a sign was put up
for sale with their words about the existence of terrifying eyes,
terrifying bloody scraps! Because it was a belief in magic, until it
was believed that the king came down to use my magic against her,
to her in her life! And in this regard, the famous incident with Dr.
Mostafa Mahmud, who once called him to make sure that an
accident did not happen to him during sleep, when he woke up
from his sleep and found his ring, the Royal finger broke from the
sole of his hand and lost part of it , and I asked him about the
validity of my suspicions that this verb is unusual and has a working
side? He replied, as usual, jokingly: (no goblin can do almost in a
dream, but if this is the ring of the king and queen, then God alone
is better off watching it). But the only thing that was connected
with this server, in part, because it is the only memory left from
Farouk, the king of the heart.

Life is unbearable .. Forgive me

Italian descent Egyptian descent, was Europe the hell of World War I when she decided that her father fled Italy with his family in search of a better place and found no better place than Egypt, which was adopted by many Europeans at the time, where a mixture of cultures , Egyptian, Italian and Spanish, to teach everyone what looks like musical harmony as opposed to what is happening now, each in case of hostility and enmity (no one loves anyone).

He hired his father in a small house next to Shubra, and this is one of the popular areas of the capital, and he joined as a performer in the orchestra hall, born in her left eye caused him to have a stern fat, ugly figure that forced him to wear thick glasses, which made her the subject of ridicule by girls who described their most violent descriptions, and her father had a difficult conflict that prevented her from going out, when he died, I found an opportunity for her to fulfill her dream of fame.And it was a preliminary step on the way by the month when the offer to take part in the Miss Egypt competition in 1954 was received without the consent of her mother, Mrs. S. Italian province and the fact that she saw in these competitions a departure from norms and traditions, because the contestants were forced to look poorly dressed ...

When she won the competition, tortured the people of the cinema with her work and met, the world of the artist "Omar Sharif", which impressed her, but she did not share this admiration.

But what was his glory in Egypt for her ambition, she went to Paris and almost returned to Egypt again, so they looked that way and made it their song (bambino) Glory did not dream of it.
And unlike what she achieved, her life, full of creative success and prosperity, was her own life, a series of failures! Married and divorced, then climbed to an Italian, and then to a young French aristocrat, both died and were the first to discover that their bodies were full of blood.

Her mental state deteriorated and she tried to commit suicide more than once, for many of her lovers, about whom there were rumors, "Francois Mitterrand" had only a feeling of emotional emptiness, intensified if she was ill when I told her doctors that she had become unable to bear children after interrupting herself at a young age out of fear for her musical career.

She visited Egypt in 1986 on "Yousef Chahin", one of his works, which was not very successful.

After the movie, I felt the signs of deficiency creep across her face, she decided to commit suicide by eating a large dose of sedative, I

found her maid lying on the bed and next to her a piece of paper written on it: (life is unbearable ... forgive me).
Robin Williams
Who would believe that an artist who smiled and painted on our faces could die depressed? The contours and hands are full of a happy and cheerful hint that the contemplator is impossible to treat him, the owner of everything is gloomy and carefree, but appearance often deceives and that illuminates glory only with a halo of fake compliments to an artist, especially a comedy one, and this is not the prerogative of only foreign artists , then "Ismail Yasin" is a brilliant artist who ties us to his films and enjoys the event and the zest, we hear the laughter of his wet nurse, in the last years of his life suffering from grief and depression, after this accumulated debt and taxes, refraining from people, after this happiest people, and he died in the end, the interests of heart disease! ..

And again, Robin and Williams, who suffered during this period of their lives from alcoholism, as well as from his financial problems after he paid large sums of money to get an ear from a divorce from his second wife.

Before his death, he suffered from Parkinson's disease and is a common condition in the elderly with symptoms of Parkinson's disease (atrium) or stiffness (sclerosis) and loss of balance and depression.

He entered his cabin while his wife was sleeping and tried to cut the artery of his left arm with a small pocket knife, but it did not work, said to connect several belts and a roll around his neck, hanged himself and found his assistant almost in a sitting position, he went out to his wife, waking her, without bothering to check this poor fellow! ...
Cleopatra VII

A descendant of the Ptolemies, and she is surpassed by the ability to thin the saliva of men, her claims have no boundaries, and to eat them to reach the top, we have no limits! ..

An alliance with Caesar against her brother to reach his heart, which would inevitably lead to his throne, knew how to curb the collective gaze of the most powerful of men, signed "Caesar", the man of Rome fell in love for the first time and gave birth to him "Caesar".

I took from her ancestors the coarseness of her heart and his cruelty even when she went to Rome and sat in the cabin, she saw her sister "Arsinoe" and sent her to the old prison center and did not move a finger or move her heart to see her sister this case! ...

After that they killed her when I was alone with them.

And what happened to Caesar happened in exactly the same way to Antony, who lost pieces and charmed his heart as soon as he saw her for the first time, becoming her obedient servant of the Drugged, and not only on the battlefield. when he caught cardia's girlfriend leaving the battlefield leaving him after that the ghost of defeat loomed, so he is the middle, and the fact that she almost Cleopatra knows the desire of the victorious commander to "stay under", to humiliate her with a report about her, and handcuff her ... and put on the streets of Rome only, and collected the asphalt so that the property would be better decorated, and dismantled it, brought a snake and put it on her chest, and in this, Shakespeare says, when I turn the cobra on her neck, on the lips of Cleopatra: (Hello, already spent everything!) And it meant death, what a genius! ..

Queen Zenobia
Known by the Romans as the "living girl" for a long time, she fought with the good ones in the art of chivalry and offensive throwing of

arrows, inherited from the safety of Cleopatra not only her beauty and intelligence, but also grace, she also inherited a love of peace and literacy. Did not find the best of the leaders of the "aurikula" his personal power and wealth, an abundant way to get more, married him and divided the field school and ended up in a behind-the-scenes government, even on the day when the "aurikula" was returning from one of his wars, he and his son "slave lat" blamed a group of angry men and shot him down, I handed Zenobia the reins as her son's guardian. in the era of increased "extermination" they even competed in Rome, caught up in a fierce war between the two sides, which ended with Zenobia being captured after she refused to surrender to a large and noble peasant! ..

She was taken to Rome and imprisoned, and there I preferred to collect fish, which the queen used to live with her head held high, carrying the most ferocious warriors on her, to please herself in the living, handcuffed hands of her enemies.

Seven Sutherland sisters

The question was repeatedly asked about the mentality of ancient people, especially in the Middle Ages, and of course I replied to myself that we are definitely smarter and our time is the best, but it seems that my judgment was a superficial bias right of these, if we put our view of Great Britain in this time and epilepsy find our all share the same approach also rally and I will not pretend that I am an expert on this era or that, but I could hit people like the one that is considered superficial also if we take a close look at the pictures and the frescoes and paintings of those times would find them to follow the same hairstyle and the same clothing design in the era alone and if we go back to ourselves for a fair comparison, we find that we are missing our mens medieval clothing fashionable and colorful, and they Miss you in the challenge and respect of the misleading male public and what is acceptable in that era, I do not find female baldness, or the presence of perforations, and no clothes to get rid of the suck dstva.

At the end of the nineteenth century, the Sutherland sisters appeared, the seven comes to see them live, I thought that the girls further, when they felt on the ground, as the rose did in the folk tale of the German brothers Grimm, depending on their progress, here is the first random real in the United The states knew the Sutherland sisters seven, and who is the king of hair 37 feet long, and in the following order: Sarah 1851, Victoria 1853, Isabella 1855, Grace 1859, Naomi 1861, Dora 1863, Mary 1865 Sutherland sang and played musical instruments, but no one really cared if he had ever played them, the audience had to look closely at their hair, the legendary female wizard.

Lamenting that there weren't enough great people on the stage to bring the Sutherland family out of extreme poverty to the rich; so the sisters' father, the Reverend Fletcher Sutherland, patented a hair tonic, and therefore Victorian women who wanted to get their hands on the secrets of the hair and the Sutherland Lothario sisters lost the flow of water and increased the family's wealth, as the sisters consider the main pages along with political issues to be serious, and the celebrity with super-rich, and in the mid 1880s did not use either of the sisters to walk down the street with her long hair without meeting the teachers behind them.

Two stories that have nothing to do with reality are the earliest tales of a thousand and one nights, she lived a brotherly life, industriously raising turkeys on a family farm in the Cambrian, New York, sponsored turkeys with bare feet, their clothes are shabby , shabby and even worse, Mary covered her hair with a disgusting odor, believing that this makes them thick and strong, and the girls learn from their colleagues bad breath, and it is the girl with thick curls that she is embarrassed among the tall grasses when visitors to your wooden hut.

At the same time, filled with parental zombies, Fletcher Sutherland himself preached and went shopping, it was Fletcher who was a preacher and a politician, and an inventor, and a writer, and a man tortured by a modern phenomenon in all forums, the work of Fletcher during the time of President James Buchanan and almost killed for his opposition to the Civil War, she founded the farm of his grandfather, Colonel Andrew Sutherland, who praised his efforts for his role in the 1812 War.

In these rural mini-farms, it is likely that the Sutherland family had no idea that the country was on the cusp of an industrial revolution and huge business value in Buffalo and Niagara Falls to be so close to centers of invention and electrical power after 20 miles. their cities. If Fletcher had always had high hopes for his children, those bigger than life would have gone to look at turkeys when they were young and would have begun to build capacity in singing in church.

The girl's mother died in 1867 and she was still a younger sister, Mary intervened in her first steps.Then he freed the sisters from the stinking oil after her death, and Fletcher was more determined to pursue his dreams of fame and fortune through the exploitation of his children. among whom were only the girls' sisters, Charles, they began collecting musical instruments to make rounds in churches and galleries, as well as in public theaters, around Niagara Square, as "Sutherland's group of seven sisters and brother Sunday", and at the age of eighteen the fifth sister Naomi received special admiration from the audience. Sing and her voice is peaceful, sweet slave, and her long hair to the waist also received positive reviews from the newspaper Rochester and Albion. Sister Descriptions (The Seven Wonders) still perform the show without their brother Charles, and arrived in New York in early December 1880, where they admired the base and locks of their hair when he appeared on the show, their first in Brad ME.

In the summer of 1881, the Sutherland sisters passed proposals to their classes, spearheaded their tour of the south, and headed to cities such as (Pensacola, Florida) and (Mobile, Alabama) and (none) before the first World's Fair in the South and the International Cotton Institute at (Atlanta, Georgia) in the fall of 1881, and every place they went there were tons of launches hurray hurray hurray hurray hurray hurray hurray hurray hurray hurray hurray hurray hurray hurray hurray hurray hurray-hurray-hurray-hurray-hurray-hurray-hurray-hurray-hurray-hurray-hurray!

Victorian women sought beautiful hair, while diseases and medicines, a bad product that causes hair fall in women and men alike, so hair became long and thick, a symbol of beauty and femininity, and reinforced the theory of the West from possessing magical powers for long hair according to legends great literatures of the time such as Browning, Dickens, Thackeray and pizza.
Big sister Sarah had curly hair 3 feet tall, her hair was the shortest in the group, Sarah used to sit when you use the sisters to take

pictures and others courted her before, and so it seems like all seven sisters who have hair covers the ground. Naomi's pigtail is four inches thick and when you unscrew it, you can cover her entire body with hair, her wonderful total length of 5.5 feet, but Mary must have been a psychopath of all the old and some doctors and priests who blamed the blame on her dark hair. adult length 6 feet. And regardless of their hair, who lose the right to try some teachers of envy in some story and stole it from the point of view of a religious mystic 7 is considered a number and England is sacred, agents and businessmen and owners of goods, they knocked out the doors of the sisters for theatrical shows of various and other proposals for your boat, and in 1882 signed a sisterly contract to tour with (display-Cola's massive), and in 1884 joined the sisters to show (Barnum and Bailey's great), used an attraction on my part, P. T Barnum himself, Brandon himself dubbed "the seven wonders of the world the most enjoyable in the world" and confirmed it with a steak, is also a journalist for upstate New York and published in 2012 a book called "Seven Wonders of the World". :

(The amazing seven Sutherland sisters: a biography of America's first celebrity models)

Explain that each sister in this family is a different person, Big Sister Sarah was the Bible with the skin of her constant companion, use her talents in soloing and playing the piano to become a music teacher one day. As Victoria's third sister, she often boasted of diamonds in her fingers and gold around her neck, with eyes as dark as her younger brother Charles and third sister of Isabella, her voice was loud, rich, poet, dreamer.
Grace, the Fourth Sister, a high-pitched singer, was the best at spice and carried on most of the business and personal correspondence. Naomi, the sister of the fifth who wrote her a sly smile with a sparkle and a Roman nose in her face, plump, not particularly attractive, was the most impressive of her sisters. The role of the sister first was to stretch your face, as only the girls

frescoes in the nineteenth century and the nose (small parties) and the face of an emotional frown could melt any heart.

Mary, the sister of the first, had eyes of a deep double, and full lips were noted, sometimes it was better to communicate with them from afar, her talent passed to pop singing and could not be relied on, and it was she who received a lot of puzzling tantrums.

Although the sisters were among the orchestra of Barnum and Bailey, but they moved away from the whims of the circus, which was rejected by the polite society, then, leaving behind the nonsense and shame, and decreased to announcements, and church music, and paintings in the rooms, and songs, and I thought America's middle class would show their awareness of Galilee, for example.

Obviously, success became consistent away from the sisters and was not enough for Fletcher, who started the Hair Tonic shimmering product idea in his head in 1882 and, depending on the last description of Mary's mother smelling foul before her death, claimed that he had invented a medicine. from baldness and it is quite possible that it was a trick that he wanted it to benefit and investing his daughter's hair is amazing. In 1883, the first trademark of the Sutherland sisters, The Seven, appeared, founded by Fletcher after he contacted Harry Bailey near the town of Mr James Bailey, who was also a big fan of Naomi, the house was to grow hair and worked on to commercialize it, meanwhile sending Fletcher home as a pharmacist in (Kinect, Ohio), and in 1884 he analyzed chemically and saw that it was free of any harmful substances, and this is the best product for people, and is honest about it. And by the end of that year, the Sutherland Sisters Foundation was established, receiving $ 90,000 in sales.

In 1885, the duo married Harry Bailey and Naomi Sutherland, and the couple had 3 children before Naomi's death in 1893, and the deceased Fletcher became sisters of the owners of the company in 1888, which expanded to include a full line of hair products, including tonic. and an antiseptic for the scalp, as well as eight shades of colors and other cosmetics such as face cream.

The product isn't cheap, with a price tag of $ 50 to $ 1.50 per job, and compares that price to these days of a vibrant week full of Americans targeting the home version of the community energy slots and the home address from (Rev. Fletcher Sutherland), which gave the product more confidence, planned successful marketing and savvy of the historic home. In such a society, a woman was expected to be weak or a fragile housewife, but the Sutherland sisters showed themselves to be business ambitions, he set about imagining his clever advertising slogans such as: (a woman's hair is the crown of her glory), and (remember, ladies, it is the hair, not the hat, is what makes it beautiful) listen to the sisters to travel around the world to promote their products, whether the hair lives in the duties of pharmacies and hotel lobbies for hours to gather crowds, in New York, for example, in the pool of the complex and to face the crowds, they even stopped traffic, prevented them from showing themselves through there, made advice to the sisters related to beauty and all the updates on the topic of hair. The company opened offices in (New York), and (Philadelphia), and (Chicago), and (Toronto), and (Havana), and (Cuba); to operate a vast network of 28,000 agents and distributors and trade, and by the 1890s the sisters had sold 2.5 million packs of grow hair unit and raised over $ 3 million. And despite the fact that they were obviously considered a symbol of femininity only for Sarah and Grace, as well as Dora and Mary, they never married, perhaps out of fear that the husband would try to control their wealth.

The Made sisters had great success and control on the front pages of newspapers, so the marginalization of some American presidents like Rutherford Hayes and William Howard Taft was all they did in the news for years to get their hair covered. who made their name familiar, add to the gossip, with the exception of poetry, prose and plays that promoted the sport, and at the peak of their popularity became a memorial gathering for them; such as concerts, gallery, invitation cards and framed cards, especially if it was signed by me,

The obsession with getting tufts of my hair got scary too, said one teacher: "I offered Victoria $ 2,500 to provide her full hair, but she turned down the offer and sold a lock of her hair to a jeweler for $ 2,500, showing the jeweler that she was in the interface of her store with seven carat diamonds, and it is no wonder that after a month, the rise in wealth affected the family and the resulting soil in which they lived.

1893 for girls of seven to return to the region to work together, and the palace is huge (Cumbria, rural New York) Where the family's house stood was their dream home and the headquarters of their place of 14 rooms, the castle like a princess with a tower, and a dome, and a balcony, and inside the decryption of guests to enjoy the hardwood floors, and chandeliers, and heavy crystal, and black walnut wood around them, the first indoor bathroom in Cumbria also appeared, marble with cool water and heated, imported by a family from Europe, so room service was a luxury in the attic, the backbone of their millions of dollars this century, the seed of spending; such as tents, and clothing and jewelry Elite, and world tours, and wine, and lovers. A virtual tin can the appearance of Christians, educated and decent, but behind closed doors there were triangles of love, and internal problems, drug addiction, and financial investments are bad, persecuted and passionate women spread news and free exceeding the limit, they are modern people of the fall, like the speculation of people, they practicing spirituality and magic, I can barely enjoy those trophies in Naomi's life a stranger in the palace was struck by the hand of death until he was forty in 1893, the same year that was finished from home.

Shocked by the death of Naomi's sisters to the core, the family planned to invest $ 30,000 in the mausoleum, but it was not built, they listened to the sisters on an excursion with Barnum until 1907, where the group tests a quick selection of physalis and interviews for Naomi, she was a woman from Pennsylvania her hair length is 9 feet, and was called (Anna Louise Roberts), the sadness is greater after each subsequent death in the family, so they spent $ 500 to get a funeral full of flowers, and a coffin, and another when their favorite dog died.

To complement the strangeness surrounding them, a French aristocrat named Frederic Castle bar came to check the role of the Assembly, but he ended up marrying Victoria older than his 10 years, he was eccentric, addicted to opium and morphine, and his hobby was offensive -shooting the front wheels to get back from the balcony of the Sutherland sisters' house, and despite his skill and accuracy in hitting the target is impressive, non-local farmers are satisfied with the professional and can get rid of the discontent by paying good money for those who were injured, and then while the sisters were on tour, their suicide of Frederick, I didn't have much that embalmed my body, so I put it in a glass box instead And after 10 days the smell became pungent and annoying, forcing the local family health officials to bury the body in their mausoleum at the cemetery (Glenwood was already at large), there it ended mainly with the fact that she died, I did not use Isabella to step over the death of her husband, and for two years visited his grave every night to be even met (Alonzo Swain) by his second younger husband.

Victoria finally married a young 19-year-old, and she was five and two at the time, which angered her sisters, who fired her, and then from the palace, and left me for the rest of her short life, died at 53 year in 1902, and was hired with an alternate name (Anna Khan) hair standing 6 feet, while at the same time elevated Mary's status mentally worse, becoming introverted and her actions antagonistic to those around her, and when the family was threatened by the spells of the sisters, tight closed the room with them, the leader of the group Sarah died in 1919, and the family again needs her body on display in the house, and refused to bury it. The last nail in the bits of the coffin of the increased ransom came in 1910, a woman appeared distinct in her age under the name (Flipper), she cut her hair far from spectacular, the growth of this trend became more common, and therefore refused to buy the product grow hair Of your sisters.

Isabella died in 1914 and the family fortune quickly fell, leaving the three women who remained in (Los Angeles) in 1919 in a desperate attempt to get their story published in Hollywood, but died in a car accident during their journey, at that stage were Mary and Grace are broken, so they didn't have the money to get their brother's remains after burning her body and never get her remains. Whoever survived from the two sisters tried to keep the product line alive in the age of no longer long hair in the desired form so that it would be funny; what the cartoonist (John Heald) is ironic about is the name (girls, dreams in the dark age) them, and we barely make a living, forcing them to compare with the palace of 1931, and in 1936 the works of the sisters marched well, but the fire lit up empty in their possessions 1938 and burns with an endless number of papers and documents belonging to them, and it is likely that the fire came from the recipe for hair sprouting, and the patents ended up with Mary in a mental hospital in Buffalo and died there in 1939, and the grace of Provision poor and disadvantaged at the age of 92 in 1946, and there was no place in the Castel mausoleum of Muslims buried in an unmarked grave, and therefore noticing the wonders of the seven Victorian titles as she was not.

Execution of Mary

It is the hanging of a person to kill another person. there is nothing surprising in this, but being hanged in a villa weighing five tons to kill a person is also a lot of strange and stupid.

Let's first learn the story of Mary's elephants, why was she executed in 1916? ..

It was a circus traveling all over the United States and there was a circus called (Charlie Sparks Charlie Sparks Circus) taking place in Tennessee and was one of the most important elements of his elephants (Mary) to be considered the star of the show.

Typically, the owner of the circus toured with animals, acrobats and clowns through the streets of the cities they visited to promote their presentations and entice the local population to do work and buy postcards.

Unfortunately for the elephants, Mary was appointed as the keeper of conversations and has little experience as a teacher, during the last (Mary) in the promotion parade, which prowled the streets of the city, using the case of war (sticks on top are old as spears) to prick her to get her to make some movements to get the attention of passers-by. With frequent twitching, she had (Mary) some of the wounds she had given them in the event of building something, so as not to break the tree trunk next to him and hit the bus on the head, and did not write this, but rather made him sit on it until death, and then shattered his skull with a mega leg.

The company was in the office, with the help of one of the trainers, a car was driving on angry elephants.

The incident spread to his and people's means as Friday's wildfire crew executed elephants.

With the repetition of the demands of the death penalty and the threat of refusal to Mr. You to establish his bride in the state, they bowed to the director of the circus at the demands of the angry people and the execution of elephants ..

But was there a dilemma about how to accomplish it? ..

Several bounties were raised there, of which the amusing one, the most important is the exposure of elephants to high frequency electric shocks. And the last one is to connect the pins between them and pull them until you die ... and all the options that I did not receive the approval of the people were left with the choice of execution by hanging - this is the best ..

Already, elephants are brought into the courtyard next to the railway line to execute the elephants "next to" using a crane used to drag the wagons on the rails.

People quickly gathered, it is reported that about three thousand people gathered to watch the execution, and put a rope around the elephants' necks and raised them, but because of their weight of more than five tons, they cut the rope during the first attempt to stop the elephants, the poor thing broke her leg, but she did not survived death, as soon they were tried to be executed and this time they managed to kill her, so that Maria went down in history as the first Villa to be executed by hanging !!
** It should be recalled here that the trial of animals that they wrote off was common in Europe in the Middle Ages, where he was subjected to trials similar to trials of a person in the presence of his witnesses, the accused, it seems, this general moved with the settlers to the New World !! ...*

Euthanasia policy

The room was very quiet ... do not choose this target, but the ringing in the ears of the medical devices was growing, which mixed the heavy, exhausted by fatigue and did not sleep with the wrong ..

It was not long before the doctor was taken away to read and go to bed sadly with the end of what ended up last the same ..

Shut up all the instruments, and stop facing development, and the spirit soared high, and nothing remained but the body, which became a lifeless body ... pulls the doctor to have a cap, like closing the curtain on the last chapter ...

I have always raised the topic of other controversies that are unmatched between appeal and arbitration, support and refusal ...

Atonement is expected to find the application of a policy of euthanasia by doctors and staff on the patient's condition to stop his suffering and his pain, especially when lifting his body of treatment or putting in a heap for a long time, there are many cases of patients who remain in a coma for many years showing no sign of improvement no matter what the pace is weak! And thus, the test of time and pain and agony, the opinion of many doctors is desirable, extremely ...

Or to leave the patient in his condition, no matter how long he survives and whatever the size of the great pain, just the opinion of many doctors is the right decision. if they insist on a certain treatment regimen until the end !!!

In my opinion, the similarity is the right thing for this. as if someone fell from the top shelf and grabbed a sword !!

This left him for dead and he continued to be skeptical of him, exhausted in pain and agony ...

*****

The first clear use of the term (euthanasia) is associated with the historian Suetonius, who described how Emperor Augustus died quickly and without suffering in the arms of his wife Livia, who achieved euthanasia, which was in need ...

The first use of the word in a medical context was by Francis Bacon, who died in NA, to mean a mild, happy, and painless means of death.

Euthanasia classification:

First of all, voluntarily: it is with the consent of the patient to complete in order to end the journey of suffering with the disease, and in this classification it is precisely when the cause of death of the patient with the help of a doctor is called: assistance in committing suicide.

Which is legal in Belgium, Luxembourg, Netherlands, Switzerland and the United States such as Oregon and Washington

And whether the classification is the most controversial, since the doctor is already helping for suicide and has just accepted it, it automatically affects the patient in the same way and prompts him to question his decision

As soon as the patient's consciousness is aware and aware of what surrounds him, and is not in a coma for an unknown period, he is capable of resistance and needs only the persistence and determination with which (presumably) he receives from his doctor ..

II. not voluntary: but one that is the doctor's decision in the absence of the patient's consent ..

One example of this is the euthanasia of children and is illegal in all parts of the world, except that it is in special circumstances in the Netherlands under the Groningen Protocol.

III. compelled: and the one who is against the will of the patient and, of course, the toughest and closest to a crime ...

*****

As for the judicial institution, which includes all explicit interventions to end life, death or euthanasia is therefore considered a crime in many countries and is punishable by law as a crime of killing a criminal, with the exception of some governments that do not allow this by any legislation, such as the Netherlands and Belgium.

And from months of questions about euthanasia - the question about the American doctor Jack Kevorkian, who was robbed for eight years on charges of second degree murder for helping 130 patients to commit suicide.

This is a really controversial topic, different views, personal, religious and stolen by the logical interpretation of each opinion, so if I were the person in charge, you would leave the patient on a journey to death for a long time or you will have your hand at the end of this journey !!!

We think they are happy, but ...

Seeing them on the screen, they smile, scream or even die, but we all know that this is just a "performance", but behind the mask of performance and pseudo features, there are stories and feelings, and louder than we expect ... from there is no way out of these stories, and no author goes over time to secrets that are secret and confusing.

Marilyn Morley
It's excitement, beauty and perfection ... this is Marilyn Monroe, that star-studded, shiny blonde, was found dead in her apartment at the age of 36 on August 5, 1962. It was the death of this star that was caused by poisoning, an overdose of medical drugs, but even now there are many speculations and questions about her death remain mysterious, especially with the confession of the police officers who entered the place of her death and saw bruises and traces of beatings on them ... only the fact that the case was closed and controlled, and at that time there was talk about her affair with US President John F. Kennedy and his brother Senator Robert Kennedy .. I wonder what is the secret of the death of this star ?!

Michael Jackson
Who doesn't know him? Is Michael so loudly demanding to be loved by everyone? Jackson died on June 25, 2010, and a body scan confirmed to the Institute of Forensic Medicine that Jackson's death is suspicious and the likelihood that a criminal element was involved in it, it was Jackson's death caused by the registration of the anesthetic propofol, very strong, as well as a mixture of other drugs. This result presented East End doctors with problems that would last for years if Michael was addicted to drugs of pain relievers, sleeping pills, and other drugs that she was behind his

death, whether by his will or not .. or maybe in a different scenario, as argued by Marilyn Monroe ..

Elvis Presley
He died at the age of 46, and this is 1977. This star killed his addiction, but his death, like his whole life, turned into a legend, they say that the cause of his death is actually an unknown heart disease, but some still doubt the circumstances of death.

And the fact that there was more than one reason leads some people to believe these stories and rumors, when he entered the hospital, the nurses confirmed that it was not an elephant. During the funeral, I observed some beads of sweat on the forehead of a corpse in a coffin .. and of course the dead do not know this !! ...

Anna Nicole Smith
Anna Nicole died without any health problems at the age of 39 trace doses of drug overdose, and after that I got a huge fortune after the death of my first husband, who was more than 30 years her senior. Before her death, her baby Daniel laid the testimony, but, unfortunately, she did not complete her joy because of the death of her little son in the 20-year spring, who suddenly died in the hospital in his mother's room.

Around her new husband Ladin bread and a psychotherapist for his wife, many young people are spinning. But she was acquitted in court and still the cause of her death remains a mystery even today.

The strangest jobs in the world

It is known that a job or a job is that you find a person who has determined his future in relation to such areas of his life as marriage and building a family and community not so many saturated

Life, but there are jobs in the world that are more bizarre in terms of quality in general. and sometimes I realize the seriousness of this weird shit ...

1.hire an employee for users with teary ladies in Japan

In Japan, this country is interested in who continues to impress, and our latest installations in all of which compete in the world market in terms of quality ... in a strange act this country has done

Hiring men for users with tears ladies, girls when they cry, there was no need for anything .. fancy work on the right

2-sex swing in America and USA

It is known that sexual relations are casual relationships between spouses and have nothing to do with locking up couples in the world they make ... but dirty and strange functions have appeared in America and a number of European countries

It is not difficult to name a wholesale alternative to the idea of this function. There was an impotent person in the van, a Fiat person not from this discipline and practicing with relationships and its members to talk about his disability.

A woman who has several risks of pursuing a relationship has not been spared by a man and will relieve her of her fear of it and, of course, he says that by raping her several times to turn {the last few months of rape, continuous} and of course, accept payment for what they do..dirty work, isn't it
3 laboratory name luxury
Imagine that your job you are taking, of which your monthly salary is to lie on your bed and live luxuriously all day from 10 am to 6 pm..it is correct, but that is exactly what happened to a university student {Roy balancing material was} in

The University of Birmingham, which was limited to lying on as well and suggested the company {Simon Horn} to identify customers to buy the bed and shows Roy the balances of thousands of euros per month..easy job, right?

4-eating candy

If there is a function limited to eating candy pieces, {will of Harry} is just a good example of this function, who is still a student at a school where his job is limited to sitting at his desk and eating a piece of candy you give him to taste and quality. light work but will cause a lot of blood sugar

5 game world of wahcraft

Lie down with your family and eat {world of wahcraft} lollipops for four hours a day, the only problem is that the requirements of this job are a little more complicated because you have to collect 200 gold coins in the first one and access # 80 through two weeks to become qualified for this job.

6 laboratory water games

Many people dreamed of getting 29 years to work, because all that is required of you is to travel for games anywhere in the world to experience salt water where required, test and try it on yourself to judge their quality and make sure in height, speed and amount of water, as well as dimensions according to the rule obtained from the above.

7.Bike photographer on Google Maps
The higher Google nominates a group of people who are fortunate enough to have users circling with their bikes at Monday locations and tourists to take pictures of places that cannot afford cars to get into them to be placed on Google Maps.

8.Guarding Buckingham Palace

Download this position as the title of the worst job in the British army because you have to stand for hours without moving or even smiling Bejaia these are the parameters you have to look your best of all time.

9 laboratory deodorants

Say the work sucks a little because by this post, I sniff the volunteer link all day to make sure the deodorants are effective.

At the end of the day we say that whatever the beginning of some strange posts, I believe there are jobs in the world that I got the title of the strangest jobs in the world, how creepy it is.

Heroes of the Human World John Christine

The waters of the Pacific Ocean shimmer, shining under the sun from across the endless seas

In the western region of the United States, the Golden State is also called the state (California) in particular, the city (San Francisco), and

Among the trees and bushes, among the flowers of an amber-bright square house ...

The doors of the house are shaking from the high noise and the lyrics of sadness emanating from the father's nozzle:

"You dumbass, you're going to kill me for not finishing the weather!

Her female voice and sorrow;

Now leave this boy, what is his fault. his meddling in your little cunning, huh?

"Listen to me well honey, this is the last decision I have, I have to put a spell on (John)!

The father raised his hand to push the mother to the ground unconscious, (John's) fear B's gaze at the signs of the face that bear the age of nine, the father's movement, his paving fingers, raising his son to Earth calmly, and the author of four candles from the corners claimed his circle its builders.,

From a hidden manuscript, old-fashioned, with the mark of the four dragons in the corners and in the center of the box?

Yen puff redolent skirts ask you to step into this yen body now, and

Father did not echo, these words are mysterious, dark clouds envelop the city of San Francisco

Picked up the ground inside the house, from which four masked men come out, in Black - these are their mouths, and

They were looking for a child inside the seal and said with one voice: a: {generate a lot of new things}, then, then, then

They raised four hands to dispose of her black can energy in the child's body, and

Look, John is tormented by the cobwebs freely: give them, Dad, please, they are alone too,

- Father cries: forgive me, Darling, I can't get away from this.

The human world John Christine / milk first class
People dressed in Black appeared
Having completed the black energy to flow into John before the threshold of awareness, they looked at the four men with their father

They spoke in one voice: Thank you, leader, for what you have done, and asked your boss about his troubles,

- But I did what you told me to do?

It was time to return to the leader !! The movement of their hands four of them even tore the father's head from the body

Fly through the air, smile, smile alone, they say; he will not return, one must not return, and the earth will disappear under the rock in the blink of an eye !!

He woke John up with his absence, which lasted all night, and found himself standing in front of the building to take care of the orphans, and that he was awake.

Where I live in a room in the Meeting for the start of his childhood, and the strangest thing is that no one hugs John from the families that come daily, and

John grew up in alleys and alleys where everyone who worked there loved him,

But John knows that he is different from the rest of the network because that night, darkness was still the focus of his memory, and

Put some jam into the milk mold, and you have a big candle, and,

- Nanny, big, happy birthday, dear, I have already reached my twelfth year, I have become a young man, baby,

This is John; thank you, aunt humor I remember so much this year on your birthday, and

Picking up the jam and they sing to John on his birthday, it's time to extinguish the sun to stop John, even put out the candle until he fell unconscious and bleed from his nose, and
Estes John found himself in one of the hospital chambers ... called a voice whispering behind the curtains

Between the doctor and the pilot, Dan,

"Are you sure what you say, doctor?"

- Yes, unfortunately, the analysis was carried out several times, but the result was negative

- What does all of this mean?

The disease (cancer) has affected most of his lungs. the problem is that surgery is dangerous now, we need to re-evaluate the treatment now

John loudly - that you are talking about cancer, any disease, any lung, that you are talking about cancer.

For the doctor and nanny Dana to come out from behind the curtain.

Nanny Dan: No honey, don't worry, it's a minor illness and will be the best

Doctor: Miss Dan, we can't hide it ... you must know that his condition will worsen over time, treatment is inevitable, my son John, you have lung cancer and you must know that I need your willpower. until we start treatment now.

Series of heroes of the human world.
John Christine second episode

This, then, then
The doctor told John about his condition and John's passing
John (in a sad voice, and his eyes are full of two tears): Am I really going to die?

Dr.: No son, get it into your head that there are many people who have completely recovered from this disease.

We do not want any disappointments or self-doubt, you will make us feel your highs more until we start.

In the meantime, the underworld reigns under the hollow lands, in the arid desert.

Knocks on the door.

- From there?

"I understand, boss.

- What need?

"I am transferring energy (pregnant dragons), sir.

- Hot ghetto, but what is the name of the case?

- I think his name is (John and Christine), sir!

- Unfortunately, this guy, is he some ...

Your task is to make you and the motorcycle Proteus and the music to this attention after that

"Okay, sir, as ordered.

{Trees and holes, Proteus motorcycle and music} these are the four who put their energy into June ,,

Series of heroes of the human world.
John Christine second episode
This, then, then
Is the leader of the underworld to bring energy .. John, because he will soon die ..
Dan: Dear John, when we found you outside the orphanage door, she was next to a box with a message from your mother.

John: What's in that message, Dan?

Dan: I never opened the message, waited a bit for her to grow up, and I think it's about time.

John: where is she, aunt?

Nanny Dana: she is in my room, when we get to the shelter she will make you tell them about it yourself, and I know, John, whatever you write in that letter, you will remain a dear little child to John in my eyes, and your parents, maybe they will

"I don't want to know anything about them," John interrupted nervously. - my parents died long ago, and I don't want to know anything about them.

In the House of Rights, so as not to stir up the news with John, I decided to focus on caring for orphans, adapting to John's treatment, full recovery, and continuing my college studies.

Knock on the door ..

John: go on.

Nanny Dan: Here's a message for you, honey, Now I have some things to do, and you rest, because tomorrow we have an appointment with the doctor.

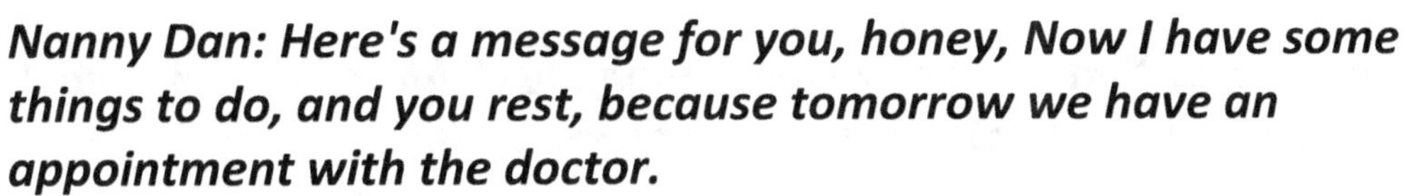

John: Thanks for YOUR interest in me.

{Calmly open the message to Christine and his heart will beat faster, then harder ..}

His eyes filled with a tear and took away from her a tear of pain, sadness and shame.

He also grabbed the letter: "Where are you, mom?

Forbidden love of the scarlet peacock

In one of such beautiful palaces and in the Zoho Best office on Monday, wag it while sitting at a desk, leaning back reverently, you should stand looking at a young man in his prime, look restore the numb

- Back, what did you say, boy?

- I want to marry Janet Brock from New York.

- I will accept that you are younger than my children, and I will not agree to marry the daughter of Leonardo's eyes.

- Dad, please, I have been telling the history of this land for more than a hundred years, why the dispute is still based on the fact that you want it to be funny how I will marry Janet and her father.

"I swear I didn't leave that bitch a dime of my money.

Julian sighed with pain of mind and paint, and the voice said fractal: I wanted to hear your blessing in my marriage, but what can you do about your money, I want not money, but happiness

Lord Jeffrey and the speaker's tone: go to hell, you and Janet don't count, when you go bankrupt, you won't take it, you are ungrateful

Sighing Julian and stop starring the headlight and Dark and his two sharp eyes went to the door and he did not work all his attempts to make his father admit failure every time he says his father's claims of not knowing who will come out

His son continued to play around in elementary school, apparently without a present, until he was in front of his room door, opened and entered, and then wiped the phone and agreed to tell her the pulse of his heart on the other side picked up the receiver

And kind to the memory of the sound that made her heart beat, and how she sweated.

Whispered the voice of the soul joint: hello Julian, your father agreed

On the other side was the hull of the ship, which Julian lifted to the limit of his anguish.

No, I didn't agree, but nothing will keep me away from you, uh-uh, if only I can take you on my knees and hide you between my ribs

I didn't want Janet to impose her shyness and modesty on Julian

- Why don't you want, Oh, my very Bella, beautiful nymph, you drowned me in the sea of love, Why don't you want a fiddler cat who won't break from the torture of my fingerprints by the pink Lady, a thief who didn't keep something in my mind?

Janet is angry, ashamed of her words: I am not a fairy, not a cat, not a thief, you really do not know how a deer may need to read some books, a passion with which I do not know how to flirt with the bride of dreams

Both bits burst

The series "Forbidden Love".
Scarlet peacock: the first part
Stop Julian didn't mistake me for his beautiful bride
To Julian: If you are the bride of a dream, then why do you think I will run away and secretly marry like Romeo and Juliet did?

To view Janet's catalog: you publish, dear Romeo

Threatens Julian with nostalgia: Well, Juliet will leave her forever on our date in Bridge City tonight.

Janet said: I'm with you in what you say

To close after both

(Thirteen years later)

The experience is insane and her Scarlet hair looked behind her while her eyes were clear with fear

Screaming with fear: get away from me, I will not give you meat, it was the Dalai Lama who smiled, and dad helped the neighbor's dog catch up with me.

To open the door of a small restaurant, a man of thirty years tall and all the stigma, she is the same girl in horror

And the date: get me out, get me out, almost bite me.

Look at this guy on the floor and screamed fleeing from the dog with the horror of the inn girl on his shoulders

She said with surprise: Daddy, how do you do it

To see this: all I say is that I do not let him feel your fear.

Girl: oh now I understand

Answer in a low voice You brought meat and medicine to the administration oh Alier a

Alier smiled at her. widescreen: yes

I entered the restaurant, simple, and went up to the top floor and entered a small room lying on the bed next to a woman so white and with crimson hair.

To provide Ellery with a smile. it was not her face: I brought medicine and meat as you asked.

I opened the woman, her eyes wide open as if in horror.

But she whispered softly: "Thank you, honey, what did you do at school today

I sat down in front of her and took Ellery recounts everything that happened down to the details from the first morning to the incident with the dog while her mother smiles at Tara and Tara has to cut her again when he opens the door to ask Price's father

And take a chance Alier a: dear, why don't you tell one of your mothers a little, or you remember her under the sign, greedy

Inflatable Ellery pouted her cheek, said angrily: Don't tell the greedy one to ask me out on a date

Then her eyes widened, as if she remembered something and looked at me, her mother.

Dear: Mom, tell me honestly who you love more, me or Dad.

She looked at her mother, and then at her father, chuckled and thought.

She waved her hands and said b / y: Of course, you, my sweetheart, smiled and became even more human, and then kicked my father in shock and said mischievously: failed

A parent's glance at his wife.

The parent is whether this kind of alert does or what, Janet.

To avoid Janet's funny: you said you grow up fast, how I love you as much as Julian

Julian sighs and says that he is catching with his paws gently: Don't worry, Janet, I saved half the amount needed to pay the hospital fee.

Into your arms, Janet: you don't have to do all this, it's not so bad.

Ellery interrupts her for a moment and she kicks the door.

Dear: Hey dad, mom has a day off tomorrow, there will be an evening in Uptown when Diana is

(30:11)

The phone rang of the parents' family religion, and then after a few words on the phone, Alier came down the stairs, lazily avoiding the phone and going down to us - this news freezes the blood in her veins with lightning and the heart passes a shock impulse to carry out towards the door, leaving behind his phone, which allows him the voice of a woman calling her but not responding to it.

The focused Alier a, barefoot in pajamas in the streets, bumped into it and fell into memories without attention and came home to find the people of the community, entered the crowd even made her way to her mother's room to find her father crying, while her mother and M has a scarf covered with a white, thin body, high knees and the expansion of her pupils and the dart lowers it until the black world is before her eyes.

(45: 8)

She opened her eyes, hoping it was just a fucking nightmare, but her wish failed

Tuesday (5:12)

The series "Forbidden Love".
Scarlet peacock: the first part
I was surprised that Alier was with her mother and she thought it was a nightmare.
For more than two weeks after Janet's death, Uncle Julian did not speak to a friend, and the enemy entered Ellery, and she is still all dressed

Past and directed to her father who wanted her

Julian: Dear Ellery, you know this is very important to me, even to your father.

And she told him to bend over her head to him and cheer him up with words made her blood boil like a fever in her veins after his eyes were dedicated to her secret

Twice some consolation for a sad and depressing day to take a stranger around the village and tell his dear friend that her father did not think Alier much before going with him, she knew that she had already locked the door of the restaurant in order to remove her tray father to the fullest

Horror elevator

Are you the type of person who suffers from the source of the phobia? You would rather have mastery over your breath, and you carry the safety of countless numbers that are being drawn into a cube of metal carrying you up and down the building several stories high. If so, then this is really a problem, especially if you are sick or weak, carefree and, since in this case you will be forced to ride the elevator and you will see that all your doubts, your worries and your thoughts are bad, you will say: you can be me and I won't find anyone to save me? Can you be interrupted by the Sling of some source with him to the bottom? You could push the door and then flip the factory and he will kill me in half! ..

Many questions hold your mind and your heart in fear. But I assure you, my friend, alfalfa, banking and the materials they put in many of the safety factors that support the safety of elevator passengers. Of course I'm here, don't say such bad things that you think couldn't have happened at all, it's a challenge, dozens of people around the world die in elevator-related accidents every year, but overall it's very rare, I mean, that the likelihood of an issuer falling down or squeezing your body into a door is much less likely than a car accident, for example.

The source of terror
Give the source that is contained.

Give an elevator between floors and stay locked inside it - more accidents happen in the fishing world, it's also more than what appeared in the movies her films about the source material, it touched non- Arab cinema in the film (Between Heaven and Earth - 1960), adapted from the novel by the great writer Naguib Mahfuz. Globally, there are many, many films that have been exposed to contaminated material, often in the form of horror.

If there is a source, then there may be a source in which the inhabitants remain locked behind metal walls, most often it is not about minutes, but many hours, so there is an emergency system that allows you to ask for help in case of a malfunction. and in most countries there will be someone in charge of plant supervision and maintenance. Even in the absence of a supervisor or administrator about the source, most people these days have devices, a mobile phone allows them to contact and ask for help wherever they are. Therefore, being trapped in an elevator for an extended period of time is rare, but it happens and sometimes can be fatal, as happened in China in 2016 when repairmen in one of the apartment buildings in Xi'an turned off the power to one of the elevators. not making sure it is free of passengers. After a whole month, they returned to fix the aforementioned baseline body levels of the carriage resident inside him, the poor thing was in the elevator when they cut off the electricity, and she spent a whole month stuck in the walls of his valve, and most likely died of sharp thirst. , hunger and begs for one all this time, because she lived alone. He was charged with manslaughter of service personnel.

The source of terror
A couple of Sherwoods ended their lives inside a factory

American married couple Sherwood and Caroline have lived happily together for six years in a beautiful home and a quiet location on three floors located in the state of Georgia, whose laws provide for the presence of a telephone inside every elevator, whether in a commercial building or residential. The old couple was supposed to have an elevator in their house and the factory is equipped with several telephones, but unfortunately it was not tied with a wire, so the couple could not ask for help when you give them an elevator between the first and second floor on one day in 2010 of the year . And no one made it to the couple until after the days passed when a noted newspaperman said they hadn't gone out to get the daily newspaper since he told police he had come into the house and searched it to find the bodies of the couple. as they sit face to face with the Egyptian unemployed, the coroner said the couple died of intense heat four days before their bodies were discovered.

The story of the American Nicholas White is the most famous of the stories of the protest inside the bank, because the surveillance camera recorded their suffering in full. Nicholas worked in one of the skyscrapers in New York. And when the spiral of his past ended at eleven o'clock in the morning on October 15, 1999, one of the elevators quickly headed out of the building, but due to a power outage, the elevator stopped between the 13th and 14th floors. Nikolai asked for help several times, without an answer, oddly enough, the elevator was equipped with a surveillance camera, but none of the security guards in charge of the building noticed Nikolai's presence only after 41 hours, about two days. I suffer a lot with Nikolai after a 3-minute video clip was filmed on YouTube, depicting a snapshot of the young man's suffering during his long detention inside the bank.

The incidents of plant material trapped inside are numerous, to be sure that what we have mentioned is only the tip of the iceberg, but more of these incidents are terrifying. that's what he gave us the director, screenwriter and early Em. Shyamalan's Night in the 2010 film Devil, which was a big hit at the box office. The plot simply revolves around five strangers swarming inside the elevator, one of them is a devil disguised as a man, the story is fictional, of course, interspersed with a lot of blood and horror, but the interests of the world are not devoid of true stories about sex, ghosts that suddenly appear to carry terror inside the elevator. The story of a bride abandoned at a does hotel in Texas is one such story, they say that the bride committed suicide by hanging herself in the bargaining room located on the ninth floor, ten from the hotel because her fiancé was not present, I received her in the thirties of the last century, and yet today strange and mysterious things happen on this floor, guests complain that they hear people speak in a whisper, and a voice playing the violin slips from somewhere, there is a crying girl, sounds like as if they were coming from the next room, claiming that some of them were asleep, when I felt someone clicking on their shoulder with his finger awake to find that they were alone in the room and there was no other person with them. All the more casual and mysterious they are, those that speak of the problems of a girl wearing a white wedding dress - this is an old-fashioned way out of the source to disappear into the corridor in front of him. It is worth noting that the hotel is old, dating back to its creation by law, 1912. He offers a YouTube video that depicts the mysterious elevators on the ninth to tenth floor moving and closing and opening the madman on their own.

In the US state of Illinois, there was a strange police report that in 2012 workers at the Coronado accident site, due to the presence of an elevator in the garage, moved up and down on their own, without stopping, they claimed that they saw a lady dressed in white through the glass inside the elevator ... The company answered the call and headed to the garage to discover that the source was already moving, for some reason, but they never found any trace of the woman inside. Working in the theater confirmed that the company is in trouble, with many ladies in white robes walking around the theater where he is said to be harassed.

Perhaps the story of Canadian Eliza Lam is the strangest and most mysterious of all elevator stories, where her body was found naked inside a cistern of water in one of the oldest and largest hotels in Los Angeles, last seen in an area located inside one from the interests of the hotel, where she began to behave so strangely that this article caused rumors and hypotheses about the girl's death remained a mystery, unsolved to this day, we referred to the story in full, you can read all at the following link: (black water .. an incredible story, but true).

There is also the story of the ghost side of the girl, the Girl, ridiculed by her colleagues and promised to the students to cry freely, and the severity of the vulnerability in the bank and then bending her body in tears without that part of her body still outside the factory, Feng refers to the door and moves the elevator to the top categorically of her head and arms, for years people have said that they hear a girl crying inside an elevator caught students when they are alone inside it. In fact, actually I do not know how true this story is, but I know that such incidents did occur in many parts of the world ... yes, the plant can be cut in half and the head of the body, and this is an example of some of the incidents. In 1995, there were several people who were traveling in an elevator in a large shopping center in New York City, it was hard for them from the first floor to the second, due to a failure that happened with the source, it was not available right in front of the second floor door, since part of it was slightly above the level of the door, volunteer James Godfrey, to help women leave the factory, used his body as a barrier to keep the door open, he succeeded in his quest, but the elevator suddenly moved, trying to pull his body out, but his head got stuck at the door, and quickly rolling the head of the gallant man, when the ball inside the factory in the shadow of his body flew out, two men appeared inside the bank, one of whom said: "I cannot erase this scene from my memory, The head was acceptable on earth without a body phone still stuck in my ear. "

In New York also in 2016, try a young Stephen Brown to help the girl get out of the elevator, but what left the girl even edited the source, so he is between the door and the wall behind the screams and moans of pain, other passengers tried to help him, but to no avail as his last breath before them was his last words that he wished them a happy New Year.

One piece of advice, dear readers, if you give the source, so don't try to be a hero or a gentleman, and then you don't put your hand, leg or head between the door covers .. unless you are in a hurry to get out of this world from the picture.

The source of terror
He gets the image from the factory surveillance camera to a Chinese student .. the video is available on YouTube, but I didn't want to upload it to my website

A similar incident happened with Chinese students, but this student was not trying to help anyone, he just wants to get out of the elevator, when you move the elevator and press his body to death, the surveillance camera recorded the slow death of the company that posted the article on YouTube.

The source of terror
The surgeon is here .. cut off your head

The surgeon here needs a decryption of matter to enter one of the elevators in the hospital where he works, when you move the elevator without warning, the door is tightly closed, here they tried to free themselves, but to no avail, and then move the elevator up, cutting his head in half and tearing it apart the body, the view was terrible and bloody, the only witness to this terrible sight was the nurse of bad luck, she just happened to be inside the bank, she spent several hours with the upper half of her head here to allow the attendants to get out of the elevator.

The source of terror
Betty Oliver, she has nine lives! ..

Escalator accidents are not limited to detaining him and his passengers, but also falling and, the chance of metal moving the elevator up and down can be interrupted, and this is rare, especially in modern elevators where there are many metal cables, the brakes of which are assigned to the source and prevent it from falling in an elevator, unless the source is very old and not maintained for a long time or exceeds the amount containing the source before a devastating accident, as happened in the reality of the World Trade Center in New York in 2001, where An estimated 200 victims died while inside the elevator, which many of them take down to their passengers. And so it happened in 1945, when he collided with an American aircraft of the type (B-25) of the wrong make in New York. The control tower warned the pilot about landing due to thick fog, but the pilot decided that, although the landing was lost due to lack of visibility, and his plane on the north side of the famous skyscraper, namely between 78th floor - 80th, this led to the risk of fire and a huge hole in the building's hull and 40 people died, dozens were also susceptible to wounds and burns of varying severity, but they survived, perhaps the most famous of them, Betty Lou Oliver, who was on the fifth floor and in the seventies when the plane collided with the building of my house, she was injured and subjected to fire and tried to evacuate the firefighters through the elevator, not realizing that the sling factory was badly damaged due to the accident, and they closed the door until they identified the source in my house from a height of 75 meters. the floors must have collapsed, naturally, the general amazement was caused by the civil defense directed by the house among the debris of the elevator and ropes and chains, and she is still alive, she was miraculously saved, For many years they carried the pointer to the stars from the top of the free fall of the elevator.

The source of terror
Disaster of the empire .. the rupture caused by the plane in the building

Elevator accidents include murderers and serial killers as well, since it is easy to scare a victim in an elevator where it is impossible to escape, in addition to possessing an element of surprise, perhaps the story of the Korean girl Hiroko is a good example of this kind of crime.

Hiroko was a nineteen-year-old student living in an apartment on the fourteenth floor. the building is old. Once, having forced Hiroko to linger in the university library until late, she had to submit a research project the next day, and Hiroko, to the architecture inhabited by them, attributed the first to the eleventh night.

The source of terror
A young man entered the bank and suffocates from lack of air

There was a street behind the car completely empty of passers-by and there was silence, a heavy one hung over the entrance to the building, sadly dimly lit, Hiroko felt ashamed, there were rumors about the presence of a psychopathic killer chasing girls in the area, she walked to the elevator and entered it, until she pressed the button for the fourteenth floor, and her heart was pounding. But before the elevator door closed, out of the blue, a handsome young man appeared, put his hand on the door to wake him up, then entered breathlessly, the young man challenged Hiroko and asked her, "Do you live on the fourth tenth floor?" ...

The girl answered in the affirmative, said: "I live on the twelfth floor." Then press the button for the twelfth floor.

Hiroko felt some relief from the presence of this tea, elegant and beautiful with it at the source, as the source crosses the floors one by one, Hiroko looked at the screen, he is really beautiful !, can you be interested in dating? Hiroko asked herself.

Finally the elevator came to a stop on the twelfth floor, I turned the screen to Hiroko and told him, "Bye .. See you later."

The intermediary girl replied: "Yes, bye .. See you later."

The source of terror
I'm waiting for you upstairs! ..

Everything was normal here, the linear screen was outside the elevator, and the door was about to close when suddenly turning towards Hiroko, clutching a long knife in her hand, changed everything completely, a mad grin appeared on his face, and his eyes sparkled strangely, it was clear that the young man was suffering from mental problems , and he did not say only one phrase: "I'm waiting for you upstairs!" .. And then he ran to the stairs leading to the fourteenth floor. The source can now move, she tried in vain to stop Hiroko or make him bleed down, but it failed, it took only seconds to appreciate the Madman Ripper who waits above.

The next morning, it was discovered that Hiroko was restricted from working in the factory, she received several stab wounds and bled to death, the girl told the police about the crazy guy, then aspirated, and, unfortunately, they never caught her killer, and he still practicing his crazy girl game to this day.

Is this story true? I don't know, I say that too .. it's not strange and not uncommon, as you might think, dear reader, the world is teeming with criminals of all shapes and types. In New York, there was one of the ladies who was riding the elevator towards her apartment in a residential building, when the elevator went up to the desired floor and opened the door, I was surprised to see Ms.

man standing at the door of the bank holding the fuel pump. the guy doused the car with fuel and then set fire to her body and ran away, died, Mr. content inside the plant was filmed by the barbecue it is completely surveillance cameras.

In general, there is a lot to say and call him to the source material, but frankly tired, so I want you, dear reader, in the supplement you submitted to tell me if you have an elevator phobia? What have you been through in your life? Do you need three strange or tragic or scary ones related to the source material? ...

Titanic 2: an invitation to beauty or a return to the past?

Cliff Water australian billionaire owner of crazy ideas will be announced to begin the journey to the fact that with the new requirements of modern time-frequency current and that the requirements for the development of prevention and the provision of social services, not only this, but also Cliff's thoughts on the practical side of investment, combined with creative reminiscences and nostalgia like April "1912" the day Titanic took from Southampton to New York across the Atlantic Ocean before diving in. The fate of a ship that does not sink.

Titanic 2 .. Call of beauty or return to the past?
Australian millionaire wants to build a ship with new materials
The question that struck me was how would he feel like a passenger
this time?

For example, if I were in cohorts traveling, no doubt my mind would swing between enjoying the thrill of the event and satiety, I would haunt the ghost of "Jack" in a patchwork quilt that moves around poker tables that miss beds and chairs inside a second class basement.

It goes without saying that looking for the traits of a "rose" among teenage girls in boring etiquette inside restaurants, I dare to storm the cockpit, and then in surprise on the floor take a selfie with the skipper, the owner of the beard, his gray hair women and when I finish walking back through the main corridor idly by ... for the members of the group who pulsate inside them and play, hearts see frozen you know their little patience and calmness can explode in the end in front of them a hurricane breaks the violin and bowstring .. Since I am not a woman, if the child did not survive, then my search to verify the availability of lifeboats is sufficient to accommodate everyone at the state level, and in practice of bribery, when that.

Titanic 2 .. Call of beauty or return to the past?
Definitely gathered in memory of Jack and the rose in the minds of travelers ..
Cliff's journey "2018" will become normal consumption for the "multiplayer .. give" category, who do not buy Napoleon's laces for millions of dollars, buy beautiful gold and acquire everything and everything and in the latter do not care about anything .. unlike "free "conditions like me, if they are lucky with some tears of madness, they will make sure that the Watchtower's aversion covers the Titanic, which the ship itself designed."

Cliff Waters, who opened the Jurassic Park dinosaur garden, trying to broadcast the virtual life of a group of dinosaurs, the mechanism did not cut his throat first and today threatens the world travel of the then titanic mother.

Kumasi Devil Hybrid

- Devil: Sir Lucifer ... brought you bad news.

- Lucifer: what is the price of this news?

- Devil: I'm usually Kumasi!

Lucifer speaks on the wheel and sends demons of communication to the rest of the princes of demons so that they come out of their fear suddenly!

Meet the devils in a large room in the middle of hell.

Kumasi devil hybrid solutions first, and,
Order Lucifer .. to meet with the leaders of the demons ..
One of the demons speaks and has been named Lord two.

- Lord two: why have you called us today, O Lucifer?

- Lucifer: I gathered you today to say that Kumasi is back.

Stop all the demons of them scared and evil, those who do not hate Kumasi

- Lord two: but what about back? It's impossible! ! !

- Lucifer: I don't know how, but, of course, he did not come to good.

And all of a sudden, for no reason! Turned all the flames that are thrown out of the grooves to black! ! And the demon's back turns black in the center of the hall and laughs with a laugh of evil, and the hall shakes with it.

Many devil kings who were born in the living room escaped after seeing them for the devil

- Said the devil in his own voice, terrible, which kills hearts with his tone.

I am Kumasi .. I am the king of your next

And then disappear into smoke.

- Lucifer: now you believe me? I told you that this can happen, what should we do now?

- Said one of the older demons: I think that we have no choice but to go to the fire department and from there we can lock Kumasi for me forever and ever.

I ended up with a meeting that has not yet been approved by all the demons on this idea.

- Said Lucifer to his servant ..

Kumasi devil hybrid solutions first, and,
Kumasi appeared suddenly, and he promises the demons that he will be king, can he?
Lucifer: Send this fund to the fire department before dawn because this fund is the only one who can be imprisoned in Kumasi prison.

- Server daemon: why fund it ?? All demons know, in a circle of people with no hope of getting out of them

- Lucifer: Don't forget the Kumasi hybrid, and we can't keep the demon hybrid in the circle of people.

- Server demon: ok sir, I'll send the foundation.
- Lucifer: Send this foundation to the fire department before dawn because this foundation is the only one who can be imprisoned in Kumasi prison.

- Server daemon: why box ?! All demons know that in the circle of people there is no hope to get out of them.

- Lucifer: Don't forget the Kumasi hybrid, and we can trap the demon hybrid in a circle of people.

- Server Demon: Ok sir, I'll get the box.

*****

After two days in the palace of Lucifer ..

Lucifer walks down the corridor leading to the document room and transforms demons to give him news and take orders from one of those demons who came to him about the danger that awaits him two days ago.

- Server Demon: Sir I commented on the Server Demon who sent him two days ago to the circle of people, what should we do your Majesty after that?

- Lucifer: nothing .. the plan is going as planned, exactly.

- Server: pardon my curiosity, my lord, but could you install this server or take it out ?!

- Lucifer: why should I leave this filth? He was ready to teach within the circle if he was afraid why he left the fund.

- Forgive my ignorance, but you did not tell him that he would return.

- Lucifer: of course, talking to me like that, why do you think that this scum is useless?

- Excuse me, Your Majesty, I will go.

- Lucifer: did I tell you to go?

- Forgive me, Milord, say what you like.

- Lucifer: Pass this message to Lord Two without seeing or knowing Lord Ergun.

*****

But before he had time to get out of the ring, the demon turned to shreds, and Lord Ergun escaped from the unknown and all the servants, and the corridor became empty, except for Lucifer and Argo.

Lord Ergun clutches the letter and reads its contents aloud.

- Content of the letter:

To lord two, bring the largest number of armies, you and your team, to destroy the comas, I sent the fund to the fire department, tomorrow I will put my squad in the middle of the field if you arm your squad.

From the demon lord Lucifer.

*****

- Lucifer is a: it is a process to deny one of the rebel devils is no longer there.

"Lord Ergun: save your lies for another time, I have a few questions, I hope you answer honestly, otherwise you will serve yourself.

Who is Kumasi? And why did you call the Council meeting two days ago? Is it because the devil is black? Why don't you use your magic? But before you answer these questions, before you come to one of your peers to tell you the news, I will tell you now, two minutes ago, a demon named Kumasi to destroy a village, from one village sex black skirts (from most powerful races of demons.)

World Series Madness is Scary
Kumasi devil hybrid second episode
Sexy dragons are black of the most powerful demon types
- Lucifer: what? How so?

Lord Ergun: You are using your magic, Mr. Red.

Now answer my questions ..

- Lucifer: It seems inevitable because of this, I want to tell you the whole story of Kumasi.

In a darkness as black as the color of Kumasi, gloomy, she was tanned, she was the mother of a Kumasi man in the best days of her life, and after a long struggle, a fateful day came, in a leap year with a red moon emitting light on the desert in the middle of the ill-fated forest, this the place of an Alien dweller that shows appeals to the entire universe, this is the place where I paint the devil star tan with the blood of human beings to come and the devil parade is majestic and take the approach of the tan that stands in the center of the circle that is available to all. the desert is besieged by a river of blood, and around a gloomy forest, surrounded by a great black fire, the Devil comes out in the best solution, and the demons mainly approach the sunburn of the naked center of the circle, then the sin of judgment must be combined with the central vocal, please, pleasantly scary.

World series madness is scary
Kumasi devil hybrid second episode
Lucifer keeps the tan inside the circle after I became his wife and brought destruction to the demons.
And after he finished, I did a horrible show of the devil's pact, and it was black paper written in blood on it.

***

I did a tanning of all these abominations than killing innocent people to bring their blood and kill others to kindle a flame; to take over the leadership of the sect through mating with the devil, and not with some demon, but he is the king of demons, but I brazenly say that I married her.

Back of the week and the Tang dominated the community strongly with a baby in his hollow, and gathered many Satanists under their leadership, and they built the largest circle of Satanists, those of the cult that governs him or the devil and the wife of Lucifer of the man himself who contributed to the construction great revolutionary organization.,

A few months ago, this demonic hybrid was born, and again the red color of the Moon in the same year, the disarming of Black Lightning from the sky and caught fire and painted a star on a bulging belly, almost exploding from the heat inside it, and from there came the most powerful and terrible devil among your peers who you named Kumashi after that devil who named Komaki, uh, that reminded me of coming, and where is this gay now?

He has done amazing things on me before, but let's get back to Kumasi's story.

Since birth, Kumasi has suffered the greatest disaster in the history of demons and humans.

Devilish music ... one of the best you can hear!

For whom not to listen to music? .... Music is present in the smallest details of our life and is present everywhere, from noisy, including popular, including mysterious and many, many other types of music, but have you ever wondered, dear reader, listen to something strange, maybe play the devil and red? Of course not, this is absurd logic, but today we have in our hands something like a date with a demon ... played with the devil or defeated the devil ...

Is that she?

A story about the devil ... about the most beautiful thing you can hear!
Just the story of my youth Just date me (Giuseppe Tartini) as a musician born on April 8, 1692 in Pirana, which is located on the Istrian peninsula, which at that time was part of the Venetian Republic, this encourages the population of this city to simply install his statue in one of the public squares.
Bred only within an aristocratic family and the author of more than 135 sonatas, this kind of instrument is based on several rhythms, initiated by the rhythm of the fast, followed by the slow and then the medium free again. Among the most famous of his sonatas (played by the devil), which we will talk about later.

He just loves music, especially violin, and has played in many churches, academies and opera houses. He began his studies and love of music at the age of twenty-seven. In 1728, he founded a violin school that attracted students from all over Europe. He also spoke of fencing and died on February 26, 1770 in Padua.

He played the devil.
A story about the devil ... about the most beautiful thing you can hear!
Representation just in his hometown in Italy

When it was just that day when I was doing the marriage work of one of my disciples at church, and then when you finished playing the hit burnout a bit and decided to take a little nap, and I made this short nap even more glorious and glorious for him! .. where he supposedly had a dream this strange dream during this dream, the dream of the devil himself, standing in front of him, and asks him if you can play something for me on your violin? ..

And he took the devil's violin and started playing, red and bloody, then just in a spiral of soul and passion, because what he heard was not something that he had heard or imagined in his mind before, it was Presto of the coolest tools. So why wake up, just sleep until he puts them on his papers, musical ones, scattered here and there, and then he himself plays them on the ground ...

My mysterious phone

((This impressed day in my life, I never thought it was possible.

Is what is happening to me real ?! Or will I wake up and realize that all of the above is just a mirage? Just an illusion?)) This is a dog that hesitated in Bali to put his head on a pillow that evening, and I cannot tell you that if you overestimated in the description, I turned my life upside down.

Until that day, I lived a boring life, I am a student of preparatory five to ten years (pilot) and knowledge among my peers, an orphan, I live with my uncle and my little sister thawed. To describe my life to you, I would say that this is just a movie that heals routinely without a chance for any changes. Just don't stop causing trouble wherever he goes.

So you might be wondering what changed my life, it just all started when I drew the phone of one of my friends, I watched him from afar, it reflects the interesting thing that I began to want one or more distinctive especially after the screams of mourning for phones in modern school became a must, then my imagination stopped fondling my mind with images of me holding a phone, wanting the league to start using it for my friends.

My phone is a riddle - part one
He thought it was a pilot's dream, but his dream was a reality, accompanied by him, will allow us a story stranger than the fiction that changed the course of his life.
Of course, asking my uncle to bring me one he did not boast, not the usefulness of the back help, The first thought and rejects the most severe refusal I had no mind to rely on myself. It took eight months of work and effort, I still remember every penny I put in my desk drawer, start helping your neighbor with campaign funds to stock up on his store, I would take the box and I feel like I'm about to I will go out, but our neighbor poked me in the ears with the words: "whoever started work will be obligatory with respect."

Also, services for finding a job or providing assistance on a paid financial basis as assistance in the workshops of a blacksmith, garage and cars are paid.

Press for eight months, I collected what the capacity is enough to buy a similar phone, and when school was over I went to the market. It was an entire phone with specific specifications in Bali *and laid out what I wanted and built on it sailed through the shops, searched through the exhibits, checking what was put on the glass shelf and did not stop the sellers from repeating the specifications of the equipment * matched * the ability hear, but I could not find what I mean.*

I wanted something special, different from what was sold by the types at school, so I came home disappointed.

I have a bone for me after all this effort and you are waiting to come back empty-handed, so I sat down with my eyes between the signs of the shops that meet her on my way to find electronics stores have not returned yet and he believed me! I saw that the little shop was taken from the corner of Place Street. I walked over to the players, selling something, and found the psychoanalyst salesman on me in the corner, leaning against the wall behind him and burying his face in the newspaper.

*I can hardly see his face. I didn't pay any attention to the fact that the newcomer showed no reaction, as if he could tear his eyes away from the paper in her words, her voice, the valve that I heard his voice clutching the pages in his hands. I wandered into the store and I understand that it has hardware, in some ways really strange, and is branded with a well-known brand, so look for the company (sample * GP) in front of me, the form of its products will justify it!*

He caught my eye, one of which was already standing behind the glass, devoid of formal flaws, unlike the others, and retained the gloss of his own parting with me with his appearance. I raised my head and said: ((Welcome to this uncle?)), The way he freely raised his head suggests that he may have been shocked by my presence and my sudden voice, not only now about my existence.

Regained my sobriety, then dusted off the paper and he says: ((They used the phones, luckily for you, I took it because I was sending her

PM today, you can take it at the price that suits you if you don't live or does not correspond to replacement)). Then he returned to the loneliness of his crime, and when he saw me, he went to the man and gave him the price of the device, which by the power of IT areas and understates his right, remove the phone and collect supplies, and then push them to me.

I walked out of the store with a smile, you know my face, and walked back to the house, and sank into a whimsical illusion of what I would do with my new found premium phone at a low price, this thing keeps the glee going and all of that before entering the end of the stick.

Age? My uncle must be on his way home. He pulled himself up carelessly and began to hurry, about the length of the distance! My breath caught in my throat, and I felt my heart jump to my throat. I don't even want to know what kind of punishment awaits me from my uncle if you are accepted.

He left me a few meters away when I spotted my uncle's car behind an intersection nearby, redoubled my efforts - as if I could do it - until I reached the backyard, I saw my sister Tala open the kitchen door from behind for me. and I entered, jumped one mighty entered the house! After going to my room, I opened the door, fished out the bag, threw its contents on the bed and pretended to study something.

At the same moment I heard my uncle enter the house and move, then I felt comfortable sneaking into my heart, but it took me by surprise, asking me, she said that I understood, however, strongly (good), if I get rid of intolerance. Only then take a breath.

But I heard steps going up the stairs and then heading into my room, panic. I think that my uncle saw me enter the house a few seconds earlier, opened the door was Tala in her head, I did not present them more accurately, as I said earlier, telling my little sister, she is only eight years old, but the problem is being intelligent and smart, they - for some reason - think that being an orphan (and something about being careless and irresponsible), she behaves rationally and maturely to rotate things of the people of the region like if it was a housewife, I think this is her way of missing my mom.

My phone is mysterious - part one
Tala was a member line in the pilot's family and throughout the house
He came up to me at a pace that was deliberate with anger and reproach, and then he said: ((What did you do outside the house at such a time, you crazy bastard, you know that if you are caught red-handed outside the house at such a time, you will be punished))
... ((Don't you)) I assured her ((after dinner I'll show you something amazing that I bought in the market)).

She opened her eyes wide out of curiosity, and then said crookedly: ((I hope I won't have something breathing and chewing like last time)) I laughed, and then confirmed the opposite.

*Splitter looked at his doubters and immediately left. I pulled out my phone and turned it on, then put it on the charger, * looked * a little at my books, and then called my uncle to dinner, I went down the stairs with my joy and helped my sister at the table monument, then we ate with my uncle, noted the report that the smile never left my face, at first it was joy, but doubts and doubts quickly swept over his mind.*

We sat down to watch TV but actually we were waiting to sleep on hooks and I showed signs of enemies and started flipping pages and even warned my sister we went up to the outside of the room and then went up to my room.

((Now)) said the entry into force of patience ((what is it?)). I moved towards my office and then presented us with the saved track and started fucking her, he put her on my lap and started teaching her how to use it, and emphasized on them the importance of not knowing my uncle with his presence. At that time we heard my uncle call, I ran Tala to her room while I was lying in my bed and pretended to have lost our uncle, and then landed on the stairs back to the living room.

*I pulled out the phone and began to check it, and having agreed on its functions, I was surprised at the shocked short Beep, after which several notes appeared on the screen in a row: ((the program is being prepared (measuring space and time) SAMPLE * GP @)). ((Preparing a program for measuring space and time, you want to register a place * of sale, time: nine hours fifty minutes of the day on Wednesday ** / * / ** 20 in the reference reference?)) Then Parameters OK and cancel.*

I didn't know what the purpose of this was (maybe some time cleaning the software or something)) that's what I told myself that they clicked OK and went to bed.

The next morning I woke up dead from my uncle's scream: ((presenter, I'm late for school, Tala, let's go, I'll take you to school, pilot!)). I jumped out of bed and got dressed, and then quickly rushed to the front door, remembering the phone, I ran back to the bathroom, threw it in my bag and went to school.

*Arrived late, as usual, and sat down near the entrance to catch my breath and tidy myself up with cries of my stomach, during which I heard my phone on the air again gave this tone, I took it out, if this observation could appear again, ((you want to record office, school, time, previous forty minutes on Thursday morning ** / * / ** 20)) * OK * and * cancel * pressure OK, as it was before.*

I was just curious to know the history of this program, I searched all sections and applications for my phone, to find, by coincidence, I took advantage of the list next to the history of searching on the Internet, he opened his and started some and found that he had recorded my room in the past at night, and also for the school, an icon was assigned to each of them and I wanted to know what happens if you just click on the icon for my room, so I did that.

If the place vibrates like an earthquake, the earth starts to fade with what we have, I feel panic and my body trembles with fear and shock, tearing my throat from screaming too much: ((What happened? God help me, Save me!)).

Turning the color all black, and then white light began to appear from afar, getting closer and closer, until the outline of everything around me appeared again.

I'm really in my room! ...
I was confused for a moment, did you really move the phone? And to the past too? But the watch showed that I was still in the case.

Poured into my place for a moment, trying to mentally digest what happened, the Shocks stopped your senses of perception, and it was like a concussion of my brain, what if I get rid of the stagnation, so quickly felt around me to make sure that I really was not completely split in two ..

*And in the middle of this heavy silence, trying to explain what had happened, the wound frightened by me came out of my phone, I looked at the screen, as if this observation said: (the transport was successful, the place of the House of Time: Wednesday ** / * / ** 20 nine o'clock fifty minutes.*

I was confused for a moment, did you really move the phone? And to the past too? But it seems that we are not in the night after all, the face of the morning sun is clearly visible from behind the curtain of my room, I checked the date and time, and by the kitchen clock, the digital is still in the case.

I grabbed the phone and stared at this program, I wanted to cut off my doubts and confidence, pressure on the school icon, so everything that happened before and then found me in front of the school gates, this time also the phone's inability to take me back in time.

He alerted me and was shocked when I found out that I was late for my lot by almost a quarter of an hour, went up to the guy and, of course, the professor greeted me with a sigh of irascibility, what then was on my mind, what happened to me, while the professor wrote math equations on the blackboard the source of the chalk creak is common you ask the same confusing questions, and left most of them unanswered, for example, what is this amazing phone? Where did he come from? Someone had to do it, he did not appear out of nowhere.

But why didn't he disappear in about the same way? Something like this was supposed to happen in a revolutionary leap, and leave all the wealth huge and the name imagined by all newspaper headlines and scientific organizations, or it is better to ask for a phone without publicity in a modest store, but not surpass the reputation of your quarter, where it was kept, and was sold at ridiculous prices, isn't it an irony of fate?

Ring the bell announcing the end of the lesson and announce that I am making my decisions, I will keep my phone and will not tell anyone about it, and there is no point in wasting my time to share this fact, it will not change the fact that he is, after all, who has not dreamed of having something great like this ?!

The days went by and I used the phone to cleanse myself, and I went from one place to another, and you were silent about it, despite the signs of intolerance and exploitation that appear on the faces around me when I hide from my place and show myself in another, but I didn't know that my decision to leave him would have a difficult fate ..

It all started with the fact that I painted the appearance of two strange men watching me everywhere, at school, at home, as well as the football team, which I should have known about with my phone and its capabilities - and hate their appearance for four days and then suddenly disappeared, I felt suspicious of this reappearance and sudden disappearance, but didn't show any of them anymore, he calmed me down and stopped my doubts, but made fun of my being, I am starting to suspect everything around me and worry about opening my phone although I really wanted to hide, so I expect to start "it's great that my life will be upside down as described, it would be so tragic" ..

You came back tired of the exercises of my team, I thanked God so much for not having to go back on foot, I threw my tired body on the bed and hope to get some rest, but hey, it was Tala from somewhere, I don't know, and started to grumble so that I can bring her some purchases:

- Come on, bummer .. I screamed wildly and finished

- I just want some food to get us, Uncle something to eat, there is nothing literal in the fridge to the kitchen.

I took it away from me, drove it out and said:

- Now you say so? I will not go, I am tired, as you can see, if you need something, go and get it yourself, as I see that you have your

legs moving freely and I do not think that going to the store next door will be a dilemma for you.

Of course, it would not have occurred to you so easily, sitting down next to my bed, but I just ignored them and did not answer the whore's pedals, which made her kick my bed with the words:

- Okay, you are lazy, useless, I will go alone and I do not need you, go to bed and hope that I never wake up.

And I smiled when what made me happy, and I heard her walk into her room and headed for the stairs, he deliberately made her steps clear, maybe changed his mind, but pretended to be deaf, which made her realize that it was inevitably, and left the house at last. I fell asleep after not understanding anything, and fell into a deep sleep.

At exactly five o'clock in the evening, my uncle came up to my room carefully and quietly woke me up, his face was pale and hard, so much so that I noticed it in the middle of the darkness, and his voice sounded intermittent, not understanding a word of what he was saying Or rather, what a word was given with difficulty, I sat down in my session and asked by the fire what he said, Were my words electrified when he said:

- Tala ... Well, it seems she is injured and is now in the hospital, unfortunately, son, I cannot tell you that everything is all right or forgive you, and her condition is very critical.

I didn't say anything or comment on his words, the shock kept my mouth shut, so he quickly got up to get dressed and go to the hospital without delay ..

There, I was sitting in the corridor in front of the operating room, of course, I could not see anything of what was happening inside, but the voice of the doctors and the drops of Tahl's blood that were in front of me gave me an idea of what the situation might be, the power might cut open the bag by young children, so doctors could not stop the bleeding, she quickly lost blood.

Bing lost hope, and the enterprising compassionate they let us in to look at her before life, while clung to the last glimpse of the little khan's life.

And on this bed I saw her covered with a scarlet blanket, and from time to time she writhed in pain and made a sound like paper, free from never letting him whine or cry.

It was worth killing my uncle and taking her dearly, and hiding my words scarcity and the inevitable collapse of the organization as bloody, but I gave up, holding her hand and stroking her hair, unlike my uncle, if I open my mouth to expose my nerves and my belief that she is dying.

I stood there for a minute and it seemed like an eternity and would never end until I heard the nurse scream, "Oh God! Doctor! He nervously replied," What? But it did not end, I draw attention to what she meant, taking her pulse weakens and weakens until it became almost non-existent, I try to revive her all the way, but nothing came of it, and that's how she died Tala on my eyes ..

The only word that echoed in Bali all the days of the funeral (my fault), so I cease to imagine how the situation would have developed if I did not understand and did not listen to him, later I found out that two unfamiliar men and a link to a store in that day and fired several shots to find out about the robbery, and one of these shots hit Tala and led her later to death.

But a man with a strange address? Does it make sense that these were the same two who watched me before? But that doesn't seem reasonable! So why watch if they want to rob a store? But this does not change anything, if they didn't, then it's my fault, and if so, then it's also my fault, because if I remember about them earlier, when I lost Tala, my sister !!

After staying there for a long time, I woke up in the morning and found that her imagination was drawing my surroundings, but where am I myself, I did not go to school and did not leave the house at all, because the theory of empathy shown by everyone will not stop reminding me that what happened and will pass again .. left me with my uncle to comfort me when he saw me in this state, and nothing happened to me, only called me for lunch or dinner.

Three weeks after the accident, I was at home alone, hungry, went down to the kitchen so that something caught my throat, and while I was there, I heard a voice locking the door, talking quietly, and the sound of two people arguing with something- then, I could not see what it was, I stopped the war, so as not to warn them both of my presence, and climbed the stairs, heading to my room to lock the same door, I heard them quietly entered the house and opened the walls of the room one by one, while the offer of my room, I hear them say ..

"Are you sure he lives here?"

Third individual: yes, having become an orphan, he lived here with his uncle and sister, this is the correct address, or at least what I found in the records.

I was sure they were looking for me. but where to hide, notice my phone, I got oysters if it doesn't have enough energy to get me, so it looks like a rat in a trap.

I heard their footsteps toward my room and the hand of the one holding the door open and jumped up quickly in response to the automatic free entry, but too late.

Here I stand face to face with the intruders, and they released me, and he said that the pilot must come with us, the whole future depends on this moment.

The Dark Web: The Black Side of the Internet

Today I thought I was going to write you everything I know about the internet dark or black ... online is blacker than all of us.

Other statistics say that the netbook phenomenon accounts for only 5% of the total internet. So where are the others that are the biggest? ..

This is my topic with you today, and this is what we will find in the following lines ..

What is deep deep web is?
Netbook dark: the black side of the network
Illustrative image for .. the network is ok .. in the middle the network is deep and the stench is dark

Who is indexed in a certain way, so that you cannot access it through a browser and a regular one, but it can do it in not certain ways, so that the browsers of others may be strange and unknown.

Divided the network deeply into two parts:

Netbook dark: the black side of the network
Armed groups use the deep web

First: the side has the least darkness or the least risk or the least darkening. In this aspect, there are websites of politicians or giants of politics and the most famous journalists, there are special locations with governments in different countries of the world.

But the question is why exactly politicians, journalists or media people stink of darkness, despite the existence of the netbook phenomenon? ...

The reason is that it is completely encrypted and not subject to surveillance, and no one in the world can track down or access the owners of the materials posted there, which is why we find that governments are also using so that the information exchanged is completely confidential and no one could not know anything about it, most of the embassies in the world use the deep network in case of contact between them and other states.

In recent years, the US government has been able to uncover messages between terrorists and one of the embassies via the Internet. This is the side of least risk and less blackness, what will be the other side of the deep web? ..

It is a dark web of a network of dark or smelly Lions, but to the darkest and most mysterious and to the very horror often.

Why do you need this stinking darkness?
Whether the black side of the grid is statistically deep is it the most widely used.

Why is he in this stinking darkness?
Netbook dark: the black side of the network
The Silk Way website sold drugs.

In the fetid darkness, find all places in the mesh phenomenon. There are no contraindications to the sale of medicines of all kinds, know the types, next to each type there is a price and there is a drive for medicines of all kinds

In 2011, Ross William Els creates a site called The silk road, or the Silk Road, a major place in the trade of all types of drugs and a description of a processed site worth over a million dollars in a short period.

And once a reference to the threat to the owner of the site for the paths to one of the hackers (pirates) of Canada said that he was able to reveal the hobbies of many dealers on the site, which I think Ross William Land is a clear and obvious threat, then he hired some hackers who hired to work on the Silk Road website, and was able to find out the address of the hacker Canada, and was also able to photograph him through the camera on his laptop. Used Ross William by another of the assassins from one of the assassin websites and with a certain amount in exchange for the murder of a hacker, a Canadian and sent him a name and a photo that met her and already made the killer a hacker, to kill the hackers, the Canadian sent a photo of his body after being killed directly in October 2013.

Netbook dark: the black side of the network
Site owner

Can the FBI figure out Ross William Els' hobby as an already arrested and closed stretch of the Silk Road, which has been adopted by many of the strongest contraindications to drug dealing in the fetid darkness.

The trial of Ross William is an earthly life sentence.

There are also larger sites to control weapons of all kinds and weapons and near their price, and there are arms trading sites sites that are often processed due to the existence of certain deals with this site.

You deal with weapons in abundance on these sites more often than not, the data is fully encrypted and often the URLs are numbers, just not Su the dealers of these sites know.

Killer Sites.

It is one of the most dangerous locations in the fetid darkness, and there are assassin websites, killer and dealer sites scattered around, with each killer having a certain price in addition to the difference in prices depending on the method of murder.

Netbook dark: the black side of the network
Dark web site leased to assassins

A photograph of the person and the address of the specific conversion of the agreed amount to the site are sent, and the early site managers only after the completion of the task.

Coalition governments always track the whereabouts of hitmen, but they often fail because this data will not be processed and encrypted, as all the assassins have fake names in the web of darkness.

Locations trade in human organs
Netbook dark: the black side of the network
Members are human and sold on the dark web - a painting for the Indians is stolen by their college

There, in the fetid darkness, many sites sell human organs, and also not at a certain price.

Erotic sites for children
Netbook dark: the black side of the network
There are websites charging large sums of money for killing children on the internet

Think of the child sex sites with more sites in the stinking darkness, where the capacity of these sites is over 50,000 sites. All I know on these sites is sex and rape of children of all ages.

Mental illness owners abound on these sites who are always looking for the gender of their children.

Red Room Sites
Netbook dark: the black side of the network
Being tortured by children for fun on the dark web ... the image phenomenon is a form of torture when children are bullied

These are the ugliest black sites of pure darkness in general. There are living people in these places to torture and rape children and women. The owners of these objects talk about the abduction of children and women, as well as kidnapped children from the streets and people who have no shelter.

And on the air, the minute-by-minute process of rape at the request of a large number of people is done for money, sometimes it can go as far as murder through live broadcast at the request of psychopaths.

Most people who are kidnapped and put up in the red room end up dying.

In 2010, part of the video of the net was published of a man being tortured, forcing him to eat certain and no one knows what he is eating, but someone who saw that this guy was kidnapped and his family after they killed his family. they made him eat their flesh, so it looks like he cries while eating, and they were beaten and humiliated.

The speaker angered many who saw him, but no one knows the source of this article.

Hacking sites
Netbook dark: the black side of the network

The Deep Web appearance and considered a haven for hackers and pirates of electronic games

There are sites dedicated to hackers, hacker fraud; on these sites, an exchange for certain amounts of money is hacked.

On the exchange, courses and hacking programs are also rare, so no one knows anything about it.

It is believed that these sites are also hazardous sites because the owners and lawyers are a giant hack and not easy to deal with, they can be infiltrated as soon as you enter one of their sites or download something from their sites' content.

Arms industry location
Websites for the educational weapons and explosives industry that are on the websites that their governments are constantly trying to do.

Human Trafficking Sites

These sites talk about the owners of kidnapped girls and children, and offer them for sale, and the owners of these sites belong to the mafia world of one of the most dangerous types of mafia.

*****

Netbook dark: the black side of the network
Bitcoin is popular on the web

After that we explained the fact that in stinking darkness there is a very important question in this thread - How to handle money or cash in stinking darkness? How do they get money from trading them? Or what currency is used in this case?

Bitcoin: It is an electronic encrypted encryption currency, data encryption for users, and this currency is traded in the stinking darkness or deep in the network in general.

It is priced at about $ 390 and is in high demand.

Are there easy ways to get into a web or deep web of darkness?

Yes, there are ways that do not need to be discovered in order to enter this world of the Internet.

Netbook dark: the black side of the network
The Tor browser is used to enter the deep web, but you enter there and may put yourself at risk

Tor Browser your web web can you to access the Deeb web, but be careful to the extreme, it is not a place of entertainment or play, but is the world of criminal enterprise integrated available all the tools of crime. World mafia, murderers and rapists, a judge, two hackers and many gangs banned in the community.

I don't think your entry is easy to understand, basically every visitor is tracked, they have giants who want to know who you are, so be careful if you want to really bring deep into this world.

Real heroes

Heroes are not only in movies, but also in real life.

Do heroes fight? Or does war make heroes?

Saying what you need to think about! However, people of war can be heroes in the eyes of their country, but they are the terrorist regime of the enemy state.
French women
A good German officer amid the destruction of his village and go with him, they decided to die for them so that they would not understand this after returning as a hero, but they considered themselves a traitor, sold themselves to work, and were dismissed by humiliating humiliation of their community.

As you can see, the conditions for obtaining the title of Hero are higher among the peoples!

- But there are people of the whole world, different nations according to the maturity of the title of Hero, just like that.

Unknown guy

Personality and source ..

Real heroes
Man unknown hero
After the 1989 unanimous support massacre in China that claimed the lives of thousands of students and protesters, stop these protesters in front of a group of military tanks in the country and it deserves to be a symbol of opposition to power and oppression.

But the opinion about his strength cannot be compared with the championship of children of stones, only this picture could be called a real Palestinian Minor League

Real heroes
Children of stones
And in this article we will talk about people who committed heroic deeds, who saved the country or even the world as a whole.

1.the Muslim hero who made the kings of Europe
Did you know, dear reader, that Al-Andalus was not the first to fall off the European table?

Then (

Yusuf ibn Tashfin
) A prince in the state of the Almoravids, he made himself feel the "slides" after using the Taifa in Andalusia and the effect of losing their punishment before the invasion of the first crusades ..

Real heroes
Yusuf ibn Tashfin
Where there is a gathering of 30 thousand soldiers, Muslims, in exchange for 60 thousand euros, are equipped with the best military equipment, and with its help I cannot, because of my encouraging letters to my soldiers, close them, therefore the stay of

the army of enemies at the end of the battle is only 100, they fled with their leader, who later died of his wounds, except for his sense of shame before this crushing defeat ..

2-Heroes of Chernobyl:
On April 26, 1986, the world witnessed the largest nuclear disaster in history, and this happened in Chernobyl, Ukraine, when the explosion of reactor IV completely, and the rapidly spreading poisonous cloud throughout the region, threatening neighboring countries, suggests that radioactive contamination in Chernobyl has exceeded the Hiroshima bomb of the Japanese 600 times!

Real heroes
Pilots and Firefighters Heroes
And if you sacrifice firefighters and helicopter pilots from the Soviet Union, who extinguished fires according to the full radiation law and prevented the leakage of 92% x, then this radiation cloud is already on its way to Poland, Scandinavia and the Czech Republic and further to Germany, Romania, Bulgaria, Greece and Turkey.

And he died almost all of these heroes after months of exposing them. nuclear norm

3-hero of the Caribbean:
Experience of a naval officer, Russian (Vasily Arkhipov) hero of the Cuban missile crisis in October 1962, there was a Soviet submarine in the Caribbean controlled by the US Navy, and surrounded, and I began to receive their naval anti-submarine bombs left and right, and worse, that the air conditioning system was down and it was warm inside the submarine close to 100 degrees! And it was difficult to sail without being exposed, and the Americans at that time did not know that she was carrying torpedoes with nuclear charges, and then the Russian commander (Valentin Savitsky) burst out in anger, saying:

- Maybe the war began because of us, we are now being cut! We will die, but we will leave them all, I will not be a disgrace to the fleet. "

And then came the role of a hero (Vasily Arkhipov), who can cool his head and his sobriety, calm down the commander and convince him to rise to the surface of the sea, and after fierce disputes between both of them, he finally offered the submarine commander to surrender ..

But the strangest thing is that the American destroyer did not conduct any inspection on the ship, I simply demanded that she stay away from Cuba, and therefore the submarine returned undamaged to Russia

Real heroes
Vasily Arkhipov
And lol calm this Russian tea officer, maybe the explosion of a nuclear submarine to command a nuclear war between the two states, nobody knows the results for the whole world.

4th American General Wise:
Gen (

Douglas Mac Arthur.
) It was important to assure their American leaders of the seriousness of the decision of the Japanese emperor (Hirohito) to surrender Japan after the bombing of the cities of Nagasaki and Hiroshima

Real heroes
Douglas Mac Arthur.
And that's why he sent 4 fighters within three days to fly over Tokyo, and although the plane returned unharmed in the first two days, on the third day one of the planes was fired upon, which killed

an American officer (Anthony Marchionne) and its owner was seriously wounded, but the general (Douglas MacArthur) hid this from his leaders, and sent in return the Japanese the need for a delegation of them to discuss the conditions of peace between them, and the delegation already visited the Japanese in full force, and he, in turn, promised them that will take the story of the last plane, coming from a few people who rejected the idea of losing the Japanese war .. And thanks to his wise decision, thousands of people (especially the Japanese) could be saved, where to prevent the war from returning, and take more destructive nuclear bombs here and there.

5-the American who saved the world from nuclear war:
At a time of great tension, the situation between Russia and America in the shadow of the 1962 Cuban Missile Crisis (

William Bassett
) The commander of one of America's missile bases in the middle of the night of October 28, 1962, launched 32 missiles with nuclear bombs. for all cities of Vladivostok in the Russian Far East and the capitals of China, Beijing, North Korean, Pyongyang and Vietnamese Hanoi.

Real heroes
Refused to follow orders and peace
But Officer Bassett refused to use his gravity, but immediately contacted the leaders of other American troops stationed on the Japanese island, occupied by US troops, and advised them to keep the missile in place.

He also threatened the soldiers under his command that he was ready to kill anyone who tried to press the button to launch one missile without him.

So this secret remained, which was revealed by the top of the American Championship after his death in 2011, and if the challenge of this brave officer for the martyrs of the world by nuclear war is destructive in the last century

6-Russian Prevention of Nuclear War:
In an interview there, the Russian hero did exactly what he did to an American officer (Pasig) and is an air defense officer (

Stanislav Petrov
In the middle of the night on September 26, 1983, an alarm went off. where they showed the monitors 5 missiles heading from America to Russian cities, and the possibility that nuclear missiles were going to Russia within 30 minutes, but he (Petrov) refused to launch any missile before reading the satellite and radar data of the Russian land that didn't register anything at all!

Real heroes
Stanislav Petrov
And it is later revealed that the false alarms were the result of a tendency for rare sunlight on clouds found at high altitudes and a companion in diuretics!

Without careful (Petrov) from taking any hasty measures, you already on the globe have witnessed serious environmental pollution due to nuclear bombs, which will be hostile from all sides to

But this bold decision put an end to the career of this officer, and at the same time to the Dresden award won in February 2013.

7 women from the ruins:
In 1945 and after the end of World War II, about 5 million Germans were killed and 40% of the infrastructure destroyed, this needed to be quickly fixed .. and that's why I started (

Louise schroeder
*) Politicians in the Socialist Party called on women to participate
again in building and expressing themselves and in promoting the
country, and a campaign (women from rubble) that was launched
in Berlin and went through all parts of Germany and numbered
more than 80 thousand women in positions*

Real heroes
Louise Schroeder women were the reason the German renaissance
New
*And with the help of primitive tools of labor, very cramped in an ax
and an iron shovel, and hand tools, he can split the fragments of an
almost 18 million building in a period not exceeding 9 months and
turn it into 750 thousand cubic meters of soil already collected on
the body of a mountain throughout Germany*

*And now on all the streets of Germany there are statues and
monuments, perpetuating the memory of women from the rubble*

Front 8 people:
*And away from the atmosphere of war, I wanted to talk about an
Indian hero (Manja), a man who spent 22 years of his life digging a
tunnel in a mountain for his village, using only an ax and ..*

*And he worked from morning until evening every day, from 1960 to
1982, although he was ridiculed by the inhabitants of his village
and accused of insanity!*

Real heroes
Dashrat Manjhi is one mountain hole!
*And the real reason for all these efforts: this is the death of his wife
due to the length of the distance between town and country, and
the fact that she can be verified by three months of government
work in the case before the cut in this way!*

But actively and by will, this old man alone can choose the distance between the village and the city only from 70 km to 7 km. and was later honored by the government to put his name on this sub-route, as if his story had turned into a movie script

The title of Hero was earned by many people all over the world, and YouTube has dozens of videos about these heroes, and this is one of them, watch the video

10-teachers:
We might think the title is limited to healthy people, but look at this guy with special needs, how to Catch a thief who wanted to steal a business.

Watch the video :

11-city of courage:
And we might think that unemployment will only be at a young age, but look at this old man, the hero who single-handedly prevented the thieves' six of shoplifting!

12-Little Heroes:
And we may think that you need the tournament to ripen my body and my mind, but look at this boy who saved his comrades from certain death.

And look at this little one who saved his brother, a baby, from serious injury.

13-love for animals:
I posted an earlier article on A nightmare talking about saving animals to people and there are many videos on YouTube about saving people and animals, but in this video we will see animals saving each other!

Devil's contract

Was this document from the time of human writing, and therefore it is today considered one of the most important determinants of official relations between individuals, such as commercial relations and general economic and social contracts of purchase and sale, lease contracts, marriage contracts, etc. All contracts regulate our relationship and give it a touch of law, and sometimes we hear about strange contracts, for example, someone doing work with a spa foundation or a university, allowing them to design their organs after his death for a certain amount deposited by their loved ones or just making this donation to help with their studies, and sometimes these contracts are funny how a foal who sold his house in full, except for one nail nailed to the wall, did not listen to the owner to remove it ..

But have you ever heard of contracts weirder than this one? Have you ever heard of the pact between man and the devil ?! As for the contract between man and the devil, have you heard of it before? Well, let's keep the dialogue short and use the following quote from The Witch to do more ..

"Thomas" is in the barn, talking to her for the black women that were carried before them, and he meets his food.

- Thomas: "Black Philip", dear Capricorn, talk to me, talk to me, how I talked to my younger brothers, Mercy and John, can you already identify them? ... Come on, tell me, do you understand my language?
Kept Thomas in Capricorn and meditated to make him feel out of your ass. what to do, she turned to change, and what if I did, even a voice came from behind her asking her

- What do you want everyone to be there?

He turned to Thomas, a paranoid hand, a serious face in the dark, and began to speak to him clearly, and again to serious conversation.

- Do you want to taste the butter? Do you wanna dress us all?

Curb Thomas her fear and she replied:

Yes, I want ...

- Do you want to see the world? Do you want to live in abundance in it ??

- What do you want for exchange?

"I want you to see the book in front of me.

And so Capricorn came out of the darkness to another body, similar to a man, and told Thomas to put it in front of a pregnant book, and went after it, and felt its neck.

- Thomason: but I don't know my name

- Do not be afraid, I will pass you with my hand, and now with a strip of your clothes.

They strip Thomas in the daytime and follow Capricorn naked through the forest, at night to the pool, where naked women seem to perform a ritual dance around a strange fire in the middle and wear incomprehensible hymns ..
The film tells about folklore folk history, for one family lived in the "New World" in America during the first raids of the British into the New World in the sixth century and the seventeenth, this family was deprived of this family from their village in the New World - due to the formation of their church in their faith - in a remote, uninhabited area, to me and tried her best to stay in front of the enchanted forest inhabited by a witch, destroyed their crops and their livestock, to enable the whole family because of magic and keep Thomas's daughter alone and follow Satan after he signed his contract to the jungle to christen her a witch ..

We do not care about the theme of the entire film, how important the paragraph above is for us, which concerns the subject of the transaction, natural gas and the most evil of all pages, the page between a person and his enemy and the enemy of good, wherever he is, the devil, Lucifer or whatever his name was not, what is the position of such health contracts? Is this reality or just a myth, born of the imagination and efforts that you put into living in Europe in the Middle Ages? Then what about these contracts and what is the weather and the parties that continue through it? And is this contract really completed ??

The incident was the largest such plot in Medieval Europe, where she lived under the yoke of the church in poverty, ignorance and disease that flourish in folklore and folk tales on this topic during that period - this is the story of Doctor Faust.
The case of Georg Johann Faust most of his life worked on evaporation in science and its study of philosophy, physics, chemistry and alchemy in order to grow to old age, then he realized that he did not enjoy something of the blessings of the world and its desires, and he regrets a waste of his life, limited by an informant, and D lot, if you return to his youth and live with his girlfriend, who left her for his research, which brought him nothing, he repelled his "Mephistopheles" as an agent of the devil.

Tell Mephistopheles the devil's agent Faustus that he will fulfill his dying wish of everything, on one condition, and sign a contract to capture his soul after his death, he agreed to Faustus, on condition that the invasion of the spirit of his project, which lives on top happiness for another, and such is the mind that gives Faust 24 years precisely calculated and perfect, will bring him everything he wants, ready money and the opportunity to do whatever he likes with the help of the demons, to whom she devoted all this time The Seven Deadly Sins, and I did not click this stock of boletus, whose fear is based on the fact that he realizes the enormity of what he planned when he sees Mephistopheles coming to wash his soul.
Is the story of Doctor Faustus this famous symbol of that eternal struggle between good and evil, lurking in the darkness of the human soul, what this conflict will be a fascinating theme of Ristov's crime and punishment?

But you were Faust and Thomas the only ones who spent the contract selling your souls to the devil, huh?

Having bypassed the church for its bloodshed and infecting it with it in recent decades, an archive of the Vatican documents, shameful, associated with the Inquisition, which the Catholic Church in the Middle Ages assessed as perfect in matters of heresy and unbelief, was released, and of the most outstanding of these documents are those related to the topic persecution of witches, in 1486 a certain "Heinrich Kramer" is a religious person, a German from the book "malleus maleficarum" "Hammer of the Witches" and this book is one of the worst books on the reputation and authority of the church. The most incitement to violence this book caused in torture, murder and burning of thousands of women on charges of witchcraft.

Is it worth emphasizing the existence of magic and witches in this book and attacking deniers and not believing in it, and also called on the public to hunt witches and kill them as the cause of all the disasters of society, and rejected it, and the book notes that the majority of practitioners magic and people controlling women, and contains the characteristics of witches and how they are caught and condemned.

Having built a church according to this book, he saw that expression at his stage is the application of divine justice, and so he entered Europe in a series of long centuries in what is known as the Inquisition, and during this period began to persecute and accuse thousands of women on charges of witchcraft. and collusion with Satan.

There have been lawsuits around in this area to such an extent that any slip or say that was out of place was given in the courts, interviews under pain of torture to attract you to loans ..

And for several months now, these courts have been conducting a series of trials on the coast of Salem with Massachusetts in America between 1692 and 1693, where he was accused of a black slave-named "Tituba" on a tip from one of her ladies, and named "Abigail William Durmaz" that Tituba's first slave was the cause of a strange disease that all cousins Abigail and her "little Paris" were infected with, where the symptoms were honestly and strangely expressed ..

She told Tituba during her initial interrogation that all she does is just entertain the two girls, to tell them horrible everyday stories, and to do as I pretend to bring your loved one has no real basis, but soon these bizarre symptoms of epilepsy and hysteria spread and fainting of a large number of girls in the country, Tituba was brought from a new interrogation, but this time by force, was tortured by the thought that Satan had given her on a rainy night and given him a book to anticipate, and she said that the book contains the signatures of some people from the country he started a series of arrests for a long time already a large number of the population, and was recognized in these arrests on two girls, Abigail and Betty, who They looked as if the symptoms mentioned above were believed in front of us that she was involved in a conspiracy ..
Choose a mixed rampage, blaming respectable people and other well-documented groups, and even famous people who keep their word. the church, which called on the latter to the fact that the bulk of these arrests was only the result of the liquidation of accounts between families and large feudal lords in the country, protagonists between their users and two girls to achieve their goals, but this was agreed after the execution of 19 innocent people who do not have relationship to none of the devil's horns, and so the darkest page in Massachusetts history has rolled.

But what about Tituba? Have you already given her the book of the devil that was promised to serve him, or did she only say this to torment him ?? No one knows.

Stay under the test, and this time on the island they cheated on me, the largest of the islands of the English gondola, where she is, and in 1617 three women were tried here, "Colle Monte" and her daughter "Mary" and "Elizabeth Pickett" for magic and the worship *of people of death, after the government and under the shock I thought "Colle Monte" that in her youth she had a cat and she talked to her and seduced her to produce those who depend on them, and he says he will help her in this, I did not know at the time who did what I told her ..*

Years passed .. he brought her different bodies and at these times he gave her a spray to see that everyone loved him, and then he took her into the forest, to one woman, she said that she could not show the angel of interests because of of darkness, and reported that she was with her daughter in this business where women talk about the creature and drank wine, told Colt that the taste was bad, and also ate bread without salt, and the king was hated in this area, told Colt that the devil offered women the book of John in porn, executed three women in the city comment the sticks to death.

According to the book "Hammer of the Witches", witches were distinctive marks, like dirt on their bodies, because they must be clean, and cannot touch money, and do not come to church or mix back just out of necessity, but a stigma that distinguishes them, even if you missed other signs, is a mole or a stamp that should be in the body of a magician and a witch of crimson color the size of a coin, and is called the "brand of the devil" or "spit of Satan", and is associated with the existence of this flag to prove conviction. Credits and certifications granted by many witches and warlocks between 1530 and 1670, and which allow for a period of witch-hunts in Europe, it is for invoking the devil that ritual preliminary intentions to serve the devil must be fulfilled, in which the aspiring magician makes sacrifices with blood. often with the blood of animals, and whether this place is abandoned or destroyed, abandoned and reads and sends curious talismans to the earth, which shows that no one serves the devil to reveal to him about the time and place where his contract and his baptism under the service will be concluded to the devil, they meet the magician at a time and place where there was no magic and witches, others who describe them. The same place where they are baptized in a ritual called "the last" is in the presence of an agent of the devil, and it is sometimes said, that the devil himself cares to be sure of devotion to the new.

This weather is filled with pornography and gaps, where there is striptease, and sexual magic, and urination, and stool according to the Holy Scriptures, and contempt for the divine, and the curse of all that is holy, in order to appease the devil, who often likes to push them to the maximum degree of unbelief and perversion. morality, and is After the signing of the books the devil of party magic, after pleasing the devil and making sure they are competent to follow it, and signs contracts with the blood of menstruation of witches and the blood of magic flowing from wounds, and is the coronation of the devil. this page to drink wine and dance and sacrifice the blood of animals and sometimes children until the early morning, then the magic comes back and earned "Satan's spit" that Spit it out to calm down, like a revelation of the dead left to die by witches like a symbol of his satisfaction for them.

Go back again to the lawsuits, and this time did not flinch "Stephane de Audi" who was executed in 1916 and died on discovering a document held with the devil and it was a piece of engine cat's skin with the blood of her period and shows the bottom the document signed, the document had the same smell unbearable, and the public library in Paris contains another document called "Orban Grande him", it is said that the devil signed it himself.

I have not included the accusation made only with devilish magic, but also include other famous figures in history, from the most famous pioneer of music and violin, the famous Italian "Niccolo Paganini", who said to play about him, it is always Epcot of the mass of the severity of her sweetness. it was about his music inspired by the devil, as no man could properly advance this path and he had to make a deal with the devil and then an indictment, even after his death where he confirmed the bishop of Nice, it *cannot be for "Niccolo" to pay a Christian on earth for selling his soul to the devil, as that "Mozart" accused of such accusations after the recital of the famous "flute of charm."*

Manuscript Giga photo:
Or the book of the devil .. This is one of the largest manuscripts in the world, found in one of the monasteries of the Czech Republic, and the beginning of the 13th century, and what makes this manuscript mysterious is that he did not know the author, and for some reason were installed, but after the spread of the image of the book and is the image of a terrible demon a little green grinning his fears, theories and legends began to revolve, and in general it was scary, but the most famous is that the monk of the monastery had some knowledge that made the church judge him to be crucified to death, but the monk begged they gave him only one more day, that one and said that he would work was not done before, and this is a book that unites all the sciences of the earth, and collided with the church because she thought that it's impossible.

But the monk is the devil and made a contract with him, according to which he sells his soul to the devil in exchange for his help in the awakening of all sciences known then in the book, so he agreed with the devil, but this time I did not write a sign, but he asked the monk being part of a book that doesn't talk to people ..

At the end of the day, just remember not to listen to any hiss coming from a serious black or any voice coming to you in a moment of weakness, and destroy them so that the agents of the devil will offer tempting offers to those most in need of you ... be careful ...

Dark ages

The Middle Ages signifies the period between the fifth and fifteenth centuries ... named after this era, the era of darkness, given the state of gradation and chaos that reigned in Europe after the fall of the Roman Empire.

Some of us know little about those times, thanks to Hollywood films that portray them as opposed to what they really are ... these films have made many people wish they were living within her rather than those modern patch times. , and I am sure, dear reader, that you are the one who desired this desire, but you will just think about it .... It is enough to know the methods of torture at this time for information ... and methods of execution to hit yourself as punishment for stupid idea ... and what he did, the doctor to the patient for thanking God that you were not the subject of this patient .. it is enough to stumble upon one of the knights of the dark ages to understand that you are a man of fortune, because you didn't stop them in time alone.

In this article I will limit myself to two points ... in the Middle Ages and in those centuries

Medicine in the Middle Ages

Ugly cruelty in the methods of treatment is characteristic of those medical eras, which makes the patient want to treat the painful areas .. including:

Dark ages

Method for the treatment of hemorrhoids in the Middle Ages

- Hemorrhoid treatment: Hemorrhoids are blood vessels in the anal canal when patients include and the talents of comitting the character of the Middle Ages, both with sharp objects while the blood is flowing, and then in Beijing the skewer of the iron is inflamed, and you can imagine feeling this sad, and he delivers himself voluntarily to the slaughter of a nurse with a knife in his hand and iron on the other hand, was on his knees to do it without the use of drugs!

- Snail: A snail made from snails that secrete a sticky substance doctors have recognized that there is no therapeutic potential for healing some diseases, such as shaking, so they sit around the snail to extract this money and give it to the patient on the body to drink it is sometimes poured into the ear to ease the pain ... for myself, I do not mind to get all these diseases and do not touch me anymore on the way, discharge this item, the clam sticky, but what about you, dear reader?

Dark ages

The dress and mask worn by medieval doctors are read to protect against disease

- Fishhook metal: enough to get Bladder stone in Leeds doctor hook metal brackets inside polycarbonate you to those stones to conflict, leaving behind a lot of pain in a position to make this patient exclaim, saying: (let the gravel, I want it)!

- Trepanation: this is cutting or sawing parts of the circular part of the skull in order to treat some cases of chronic headaches and epilepsy, and this was done with a machine metal drill without the use of any drugs, except that they needed a volumetric lump to expel evil spirits! The Secretariat does not see any sense in them after such an act.

Dark ages
Brain processes were work of cracks in the head or through the eye
- Excision of a part of the brain: in order to be mentally ill, in those days it was done either by mouse experiments, or by the most disgusting methods of treating physical and mental illnesses - the introduction of a long ice rod to hollow the eye to the brain in order to eradicate its parts in order to remove excess electricity from the brain.

- Treatment with heroin: yes, it was heroin, which is one of the most dangerous drugs currently, one of the methods for treating cough in children, and heroin is a narcotic extract from opium that destroys nerve cells in adults, so why are we as poor people? ! That filled their hospitals, not like my cough, but like fucking tweakers!

Dark ages
Children had to be cut with a chainsaw without anesthesia
- Bled: connecting doctors in those days between the menstrual cycles of women who take it as an antiseptic and for many diseases they treat by creating a wound in one of the large veins around the man and woman, until they get rid of the bad blood. which is known to be a process (of bloodletting), and thus lead to the deaths of many Bled, including the American president (George Washington), who had a sore throat.

Knights of the Middle Ages
Dark ages

Knights of the Middle Ages
One of the most famous phrases in the historical epic (Braveheart) is when you introduced the hero William Wallace to the nobles during their meeting, saying: (the unit we make, we get what he didn't get from us, we go home) .. Such phrases fireworks did to us what we can, if we are lucky one day and meet one of the knights of the Middle Ages, even during a fleeting sleep, riding a horse, dressed in armor, carrying a sword and Pica in a majestic chilling gaze, but sorry, dear reader, let me rip this picture and turn it upside down, I am reading these lines to define God a thousand times that you have not met them in time or place, imagine that you are on a journey inside a time machine, traveling in the Middle Ages, here exactly what you will find a knight there .... A man of short stature and not the same as in the photographs for you, tall, broad-shouldered, massive body, not about one and a half meters, despite the fact that he is short, but I would udu to stand tall in front of him .... Not only that, you will find a body full of skin diseases of the face, covered with pimples and sores, until his features disappear behind those scars.

Dark ages
Under this class the glittering majestic takes a man soaked in his own filth
He will smell from a mile away, he wears a metal shield for a long time, and under his sweat and dust all this variety of various insects accumulates, not only bathing twice a year, but also receiving information faster than at that time ... you can pray to God not to smile, her knight in Gallant does not even see your worst nightmare in the form of yellow teeth is ugly, as soon as you see it, you may know that there is for a week, the culture of washing teeth did not exist ... and as for the soldier's age , only three years old and has empty teeth in his mouth.

These things were not chosen by the cavalry, only generals and even kings took part in them ... the dog, not only in those cases when even Europe became a breeding ground for many deadly diseases, the Reaper, the water was their sworn enemy, did not recognize him except for the purpose of the company , soap did not know him except from the Arabs, it came, according to the description of the king of France, to the smell of a wild animal, the best of them! This situation is famous for the fact that Queen Isabella II made a promise to herself not to change her underwear until she succeeds in siege of one of the cities left to wear these clothes for three years - this is the length of the siege that died from doing the work!

And it was the task of regulating the markets and streets lying on the pig, which is made up of wishful thinking people who have been changed and piss on the streets just like other droppings, but in the end, droppings leaves must fill the roads, bringing with a lot of infectious diseases!

Poison flower

Several steps separated them from each other, tears fell from her eyes, like a volcano throws one of its hot on her cheeks, pain was considered a heart, there were no more than a few people in the room, almost not distinguishing their faces from many tears, the room was gray and the smell death dwells among the graves, almost certain that she hears the voices and screams of people who met their fate last in this gloomy room .. I did not expect a day from birth that their intervention in any case is far from the perception and her imagination of the patient , the whole story of her life passed before her eyes, like celluloid, while someone said something to her, but she did not hear him and focused her gaze on the person who was standing and waiting for her to save her life, after a few moments , and the minutes passed like an eternity, and a million times I wanted to stop time at this moment ..

Her heart was pounding furiously, she could not stand and could not be Mr. not proposed by two people interested in fate, I did not enjoy the conflict, they know the crime well and know that the price of her crime is her life, and although she knew that she should, not hesitating, he tears the MMK, and here is how a dictionary of words to describe this moment .. Now the appetite for death, that as in front of the most powerful of the titans, and down in front of him the kings of the earth, leaving behind them all, and in silence placed a noose around her neck, cleaning in order to prevent around and how to leave them in solemn silence, but her tears and persuasions, she does not intercede for him, and thus attracts (Ashmawi) the floor of the gallows to fall into the abyss, she remembered that her crime from the very beginning and it was a beginning without a beginning, and they began to remember, and to remember

** * **

Gift of sound
Poisonous flowers.
Born and raised in luxury
When you hear this title for the first time, think that the title of the film is representative of what ... and for the record did not disappoint, dear reader, they are representatives of a very special kind, come and let's

We are talking here about 1967, she (the gift of Abdulrahman Salim Amer), an Egyptian citizen and her father was an agent of the Ministry of Education, and by nature lived a luxurious life, where she lived next door to the engineers, the neighborhood that they were buying at that time, higher people .. her life was empty, like any girl at her age, who does not dream of fashion and makeup and fashion, and conversations with her with the account and women are what at that time successfully received a certificate of maturity and was one of pioneer club island ..

At this time, Egypt was on the verge of a conflict with Israel, and suffered setbacks, which cost Egypt dearly, and these were the souls of dashing designers, and although you did not care (a gift) about what was happening around her, but continued her dreams of rosacea and aspired to their achievement, and the first step was a trip to Paris, I took all their energy to organize what I intended for him, and took a tour and are available on the territory and in the club, and this is no less than they have in anything something.

And the days go by until the peeling Sur-father refuses to stick a miracle, and this was the first step at the end of her life's path, it was a fate prepared for him even more things that you never imagined ever ..

Travel to the land of light (remember the end)
Poisonous flowers.
I went to France
This is Paris, City of Light and freedom in everything, fluent in French, and that is what helped her launch this community that has limitations in it, and found that the study was different about Egypt, they are from articles that include them and when enjoy this, life in Paris was paradise on Earth for her, and that is why I did not put restrictions on him, and not for his side or personal, it is a logical layer and is integrated with everyone, Jews and non-Jews do

not matter, it is important to enjoy the time before extremes, and more and more, until it fell with them, and now bring your parties and eat their food, and through a friend from the University of Jewish origin.

And since Israel is a Zionist entity synaptic and lumpy to serve the same purpose, it was natural to seize on this golden opportunity, and the Mossad officers he had driven attended these private parties regularly and brainwashed them indirectly to change her mind and make her watch films about Israel. to see how it is a country of civilization and that the bad image that the Arab world has launched is pure filth.

And I do not deny that the conditions of this period because of the Nakba, and the rumors that the Israeli army is invincible, and that America is the defender of the bathroom and will not leave her little girl beaten in front of the designers, helped them a lot in their search, and this reinforced the image of Israel in her mind that her army was not defeated, while at the same time it helped her college professor to extend her studies in France to two years, during which time the Mossad was able to turn expatriate students into Parisian emigrants. Where they gave them money and promised her to make her dreams come true, and are sure that the authors did not consider gifts or cans of cosmetics expensive or the clothes of a translator, but she was completely convinced that Israel was not in the next episode, and therefore forgot all her thoughts, and her channel about our country, which lived and grew !!

Poisonous flowers.
Farouk Al-Feki
And without thinking twice, I decided to answer the owner of our beauty in a different way, and without hesitation, they tried to recruit (Farouk Al-Feki) one of the officers on his very first trip back to Egypt, after which the Mossad officer learned through her that he loves her and chases after her, so they decided to take

advantage of this connection, this consolidated their connection and began to use it in their own interests, so they agreed to his speech, and visited the Lvov Guild of officers, and there was a conversation about the island's pioneer club and circles high class at the time ..

I used this gift to ask Farouk about the locations of the missiles and their bases, about the exploitation of her femininity and who defies description, about her sharp intellect, about her culture successfully recruited for the Mossad, and she wasted no time for nothing, she transmitted information from the bottom of her heart, and military cards non-stop ..

Officer in the wind
After the announcement of the engagement, big problems began to open with keeping him in his absence due to his work at the front, and through him and indirectly, I knew that the deal with Egypt on the Russian group of missiles would have a strong impact on the Egyptian forces in the upcoming war with any the war of October 1973.

Poisonous flowers.
The SAM system is designed for anti-aircraft installation
She began to look for him, and simply took with her not maps, but to explain where the missile rules were, and with all honesty sent information accurate to the Israeli Mossad, she mastered the Mossad, was well trained, and although it was clear to him, she made fun of him and his culture, humble, and he always felt inferior and small in front of the culture of the West, and it was not a surprise to show off her work, and took her to her apartment to show her troops and weapons depots in front of her, and send the news without delay to France to see how they approach this tuner in Israel and reassure the Israeli side of the information, and ask an Israeli officer to take care of them and present their attitude.

And it was lightning that struck these rules even before the cement in construction had dried up, and this was repeated more than once, and the hot side of the spring, and intelligence, and they knew that there must be a spy among the ranks of the army.

The Egyptian intelligence department has big problems and speed, and they could not hide the spy until one of the soldiers said that there was radio communication in the office of the special officer (Farouk), and I do not know the reason for his presence, and in order to reveal and restrict you, he admitted in everything, and exploited the Egyptian side as a double agent for a while, and then executed ... and I knew about Anwar Sadat, and you went out (gift).)

Falling poisonous flowers.
Poisonous flowers.
Photo of a gift with Farouk in the night Saher
Intelligence Lane how to accept (gift) - it was in France - before leaving for Israel if I knew about her were disclosed, and there were two decisions, not three of them .. the first to lure into the airport (Libya) where her father worked in the field of education there, or filter, where it is a big risk, she began to freeze a lot of the Arab diaspora in France and decided to Egyptian intelligence, the implementation of the first plan ..

The group was traveling (Rosa Gabrielle) to get her to Egypt and I had to help her father, unknowingly, to say that his daughter was involved in a plane hijack with a Palestinian organization and that the French authorities would be on them and should be smuggled out from France don't even put the name of Egypt in this topic .. the father agreed immediately and the plan was to enter the hospital under the pretext that he is very sick and wants to see before dying ..

The telegram came as a (gift), but when I told the Mossad about it. they refused to go out of doubts that it was all set up, so they wanted to ascertain the illness of her father, so they sent him a telegram in Dara language to bring the history of Tripoli to Paris, but the hospital refused on the grounds that his condition was critical, they tried The Mossad took all the way between her and the trip, but all attempts failed, and I did not find (the gift), I had to go to Tripoli .. And signed the flower immediately upon arrival at the airport of the Libyan, the space collar of Egyptian officers and they carried the lamb after that as he fell to the ground in shock, he told her that they were intelligence officers in Egypt and they were heading back to base, and were waiting for the plane to go quickly to the (gift) last.

Poisonous flowers.
Golden meters, Israeli government tried to keep the gift, but late President Sadat in the area
And there, inside the prison, a special cell was allocated for her, and inside it was brought (a gift), and she had the hope of sending Israel to save her from her fate, inevitable, loss of both, and how not, and she did them a valuable service, and recruited a lot abroad, and cost the Egyptian military great losses at the critical moments of the 1973 war !!

Before the investigators, everything was thought out in pride and pride, and the smoke of a cigarette was being sold, which was burning between the whites now, and the officials met at the time of all their requests and did not think that they would even receive all the information in the best format, each stock has its own brought to the dungeon for her, perfume bottles and a box of cosmetics, and so on, and everyone knew the news about the fall of the most dangerous spy, and disowned her entire family, except for her uncle, do not disclose the sources of the name of his order, where he was a celebrity, and whether he was a guest she's not there all the time ..

And in prison, other prisoners throw their most atrocious insults, passing in front of their own cameras, and they see themselves as the best of them, since she betrayed her homeland and, no matter what they did, they did not betray their homeland ..

And in front of the judges, he was sentenced to death because of what I did, and the verdict was lightning fast no, how has he still not moved to Israel ?! And Hope began to drain, and I tried to file a petition for a mitigation of the sentence, but it was rejected .. during this period he was in Egypt, Henry Kissinger, the American foreign minister, was in an interview with a cataract, and took the opportunity to ask for forgiveness for (gift) will satisfy the government's interest in any form, whether it be an exchange of prisoners or even relieve the itch, especially that this request was a golden man personally, but Sadat had the intelligence to make his answer immediately:

- I executed

- When?

- Today

And it came as a shock to Henry and Israel, and signaled to Sadat what it meant: (The death sentence was carried out immediately.)

He was not (gift) executed after, but he was executed on the same day, and the curtain on the flower is poisonous (gift of sound) the most dangerous spy in Egypt

When the machine speaks

When the Silent Tongue finds nothing to say, sound is the best answer to some of the disappointments that plague us on the journey of our long life. This is not a requirement that you personally be disappointed in yourself, and it makes you unable to pronounce and understand something, because you are just tired of it all, but you can be disappointed in a relationship not related to a person like you who is suffering and suffering. ..

Let everyone can capture a certain image of themselves or other people or their friends, but there are some wanted to get a photo of diverse humanity, they said to take a photo at the right time .. photographed humanity said its last breath .. and in another, humanity belongs to the only one, who has no denomination and race ..

We will look at two types of photographs in this article .. humanitarian photographs demonstrate to you that this world is still beautiful, and photographs can make you share and live.
1 - Hope has risen
I am sure, dear reader, that there are some who can lose hope due to failure in some things, yes, we can fail and do and do .. but it is very difficult to treat standing again, I myself gave up so much, I don't could find what to do other than sleep and escape from the unfortunate reality, but the owner of this painting all decided to commit suicide, but God's soldiers not an American policeman brave managed to convince him and force him to make amends for his desperate idea, we see it in the painting as he continues his words Hope to make amends for his idea, and after 8 years this guy in despair that he tried to commit suicide got his life and being a

happy family, in appreciation for the beauty, we see in the picture he offers a prize so a man-officer.

2-reader simple

A beautiful photograph showing a homeless reader asleep on the floor at a train station after a passenger donated an e-reader. The passenger is generous and he noticed that the homeless person has been reading the same book every day for a long time, because he has no money to buy another book, a secret device to be able to read whatever they want from the book .. and I give for this, dear reader, of course, you do not need compassion and nothing else. God forbid that everyone would thank God by mowing and earn their living ... but the gift that you give Linda in your own way and in my opinion, and if one day you buy your course for those who ... don't worry ... what would she didn't buy the minimum in the dark, there's always a little speck of a light kiss in the middle.

3-Fire of humanity

In Victoria, Australia, a specially dill string of fires is quite huge inside the forest there, so I rushed to the children to rescue the situation there, to save the wildlife for fear of turning into ash .. and to show the factor of the koala animal's fire fall after his saliva dried out from the heat of the bursts of flame.

4-barefoot

When you talk to the car.

How many times have we seen poor or homeless people on the street suffer from the hardships of time, cold, hunger and nudity, how many times have we wanted to help them and tell them our pain and sorrow, but how many times have we had the courage and sincere intention to fulfill our desires with the help of these unfortunates ... several times, of course, it's not even that some never think about helping others, because he takes care not only of himself ... but this old man depicted in the picture has a sincere *intention and a great heart before to the point that he blows up. His shoes, which he offered this girl, were barefoot.*

5-Oh you
What is the fastest pace of days span of years, we may think that life is long, we can sometimes slow down the passage of time, we sit at our desks at work, but life is shorter than we imagine ... perhaps this expressive image is good an example of the speed of passing work, look at this little child, and he needs his ball and his father's hand in front of their house in 1945 ... and then he became an old man again, he needs a ball, too, maybe, however, his father is a thing before same home, but in 2009 ..

6-war in Nigeria, tribe for
Due to the economic, ethnic, cultural, religious tensions, a fierce war broke out between the tribes in Nigeria, it was a war of a very harsh sense of the word and left behind many tragedies and pogroms that continued on the forehead, not on the eye and continued specifically from 16 July 1967 and January 13, 1970, during these years in the crotch, in three meetings, most of the members of the Ebola tribe died due to severe hunger and lack of water, as a result of a stifling siege imposed on them ... of course, the dog followed its ambition and did not care about the damage that would be caused by this war and this photograph, which tells of this tragedy through the lens of photographer Don McCullough.

7-fight against time
When you talk to the car.
I liked that my name is that, in the photo of the name, which depicts an old woman of advanced age 106 years old and stuck with a Kalashnikov-type assault rifle, where he guards a house from thieves on the Armenian-Azerbaijani border in an attempt to certify the age of the tyrant who ruined him, and the time that will never bring them back, no matter what I do, and, apparently, the dog abandoned by the deported, and the date of her loneliness in her

modest house, but we sat with her and did not leave her, as if he had the iron heart is full of fractions, but this kind-hearted human heart of flesh and blood claimed to its companions that it was full of brilliant humanities.

8-conscience is lost
When you talk to the car.
I apologize for the ugliness of the area, as well as for turning my back on them because of this picture, which proves that the situation can sometimes reach the lowest level of humanity's social status, so much because of pronouns is lost between the darkness of the heart and fire to sweep . The image of a mother pretending to be venomous foals next to her little daughter's wound was the victim of a savage husband and father, spoken with causticity at his wife and daughter during their sleep, and all this because of the threat of divorce of his wife, because he severely beat her. I disfigured my mother's face, completely lost sight of her, just as a little girl lost sight of her next to her mother, as if saying: "I will not leave you, mother." in the darkness of this cruel life I will be with you even in the darkness of blindness.

9. Love and self-realization
When you talk to the car.
Almighty God, even an animal knows what compassion is, which was absent in the hearts of most of humanity, and why it does not change, and everyone is busy with pride, the lost slogans of Elahi, who do not care about helping others ... the beautiful picture shows a yellow dog with a golden tint, she stands next to her friend and is disabled, cannot walk, sees in the picture how they embrace tenderly and thank him for his help in most of the affairs of her life, which was accompanied on a trip to a distant shore .. this picture can cause you have pity for some of the human teachers who may be neglecting their own people.

10 Barber Street

When you talk to the car.
Doing good doesn't offer much, but maybe a little. We can also make good examples simple and do not need adjustment if you are feeding a cat or watering a bird with thirst, so be sure that you are still fine and not contaminate your pronouns with mold after how it will work a little, but it is a lot when others ... this picture shows a haircut in New York, where we shave the head of one of the needy, on the streets it is shaving every day to shave the heads of the poor and the humble, and, of course, the picture is not always rosy in America, as some think, there are also crises that the country is going through and left behind by the homeless and the poor who have no food for the day.

11-The Incredibles Cleaners

When you talk to the car.
A beautiful picture for the client system while cleaning a bottle at a children's hospital in Memphis USA, the picture shows workers dressed as khaki characters known to children and with hope and a smile in their hearts, the scene does not say too much, especially in the Arab world that, perhaps you can sometimes draw a child taking his last breath at the anger of a high school student.

12th Happy Birthday

When you talk to the car.
A beautiful photograph depicting a child with autism, imagine that his friends came to his birthday, told his mother to post his story on the social networking site Facebook there was a surprise that the fire brigade attended to attend the child's birthday in addition to some policemen and the fact that they left behind their smile of childish beauty, which revived hope for tomorrow in him.

Football .. is not just a game!

Who hasn't watched footage of a football match in their life? Who has not heard of this most widespread sport in the world, which takes people time and fills their lives thanks to its streets and corners of the largest country in the world with the greatest progress? Who hasn't asked their friends not to play football all the time? Since March, this game has not caused pain and regret? Who among the women in the world does not remember because of her husband's concern that she is neglecting her children for their lessons because of her? It is the most popular sport in the world, the sport of beauty, longevity and history .. Although they are loved by the majority of the world's population, since there are more games to achieve longevity, I see that it is not just a game, football is more than just a game ..

"In football, blind, real - I only see the ball," says the entire journalist and writer Brazilian Nelson Rodriguez, it turns out that football is deeper than just a game, and that the ball is covered with leather with dust and dirt that throw their feet and their large, so as not to interfere with them a little more than being a round figure, is a blow to him like a stray one. Quite simply, the balls carry a lot of esoteric knowledge. Why the publication of an article about football earlier on this site, that's why I wanted to trade the oldest extra short and simple ones, I will talk about the history of the genesis of this sport, or how its game is not about its teams, not about months ago, its players or their income, we explore some of

the historical moments in this game that prove to us that it really deserves to be a valuable target.

Tears of Brazil
Three years ago, and in the summer of 2014 was the World Cup in Brazil, the event is the greatest work of the whole world, it was the middle of the Brazilian tournament, the organizers completed their readiness, laden with the successes and big names that were the hopes of the Brazilian people, held for the coronation of the mother of cups, began a high-spirited Brazilian team competition against the world of the Earth and the public has already achieved the first victory in the tournament at the expense of the average Croatia with a score of three goals with the sole purpose of continuing their career with a draw and winning others even skipping the group stage and then missing the world championship. mid-Chilean and Colombia advanced to the semi-finals and sewed it into a draw in the face of mid-Germany, one of the stronger candidates for the title collection, the game was Regular on pins and needles under the media coverage very large and tight as the cuff is likely to win Brazil.
And on the night of July 8, 2014, the whistle for the semi-finals of the World Golf Championship of the mine in Brazil, in front of 58 thousand spectators from the stands and a billion followers around the world, fell on Brazil humiliatingly both at home and in front of its audience with a score of 7 -one ! Samba struck the German defense technique easily and fantastically, and it rolled down the goal in a cascade in front of the amazement of those present and the shock of the ball fans. "Germany, several manners!" It was one of the headlines that summarized everything that happened that night, Germany is cruel and.

Aspects of the tariff in it, if it were not the result of the game of his parties, are that the German gets drunk and gets an adaptation of the results in the quiz and connects 1.3 million euros! He was intoxicated and got unconscious as a result! This confirms that it was impossible, but when you lose your mind and cannot get things, it is possible that the Brazilian player was a normal pre-match report holder in the war with a vintage report in his hands and some kind of weed under his socks, because they gave a performance that was relevant for viewing dance of the gynecologist and not to challenge the semi-finals of the world championship.

The masters of the land crushed Germany mercilessly and the Brazilian who went out for seven cups of coffee I enjoyed in front of the tears of the Brazilians and the amazement of the whole world, it was something unexpected and incredible it was a real massacre of a wolf pack of women Brazilian hair then Haddadi looked like a great massacre on this defeat what happened, but everything in it is a painful loss in sports, as the mission seems trivial, everyone was disappointed and refracted. That evening, when the Brazilian defender David Luis came out with a statement that left an impressive mark on the hearts of all who heard him, where he said crying: "I think that everyone, I think that all Brazilians, I would like to see how my people are smiling. "as Beijing goalkeeper Julio Cesar during a live interview with a journalist. Later, I had almost no fans (only 4 fans), it is appropriate to greet the players in the camps, how could you not do this after such a scandal? The elite of Brazil, for example the army returning from the war, devastated and destroyed their country with him.

The sunken streets of Brazil in grief and sorrow for whole days, between the sobs of your children and old people, it was the Brazilian people who shed the tears of Medrara and suffered for their country ... this is a game, you know? I leave you with these images that sing about dogs ..

They achieved the title and became flags!
Football, like the universe, you get natural phenomena based on reciprocity and in some way attracting the attention of all the inhabitants of the world, everything will be quiet before each

football season and no one will expect what the results will be with the end of the season, for example, the 2015-2016 season ... Rarely are there big surprises in the world of football and will always be preceded by a large number of signatures, but the history of a Premier team is a surprise of the highest caliber that will remain recorded in football history regardless of the years that have passed. The team is very simple in the second class with the potential of a modest circular accession to the throne of English football, and I don't know, the English Premier League is the most powerful country in the world, if not its leader, and who does not know football in England, they are exceptional and differ in form and content, therefore it is considered part of religious rituals. It was such a big surprise for the whole world. Just make sure you Leicester City's FA team didn't step over the heads of our elders, led by Italian old Claudio Ranieri after his teaching career failed, and then when everyone ridiculed him for not having surnames, the way he told the group players, including real wonders such as professional Jimmy Warda is an English player playing in an amateur league in which he was a player completely immersed in the material and banished from Andy, his misfortune turned many times after his discovery in Leicester working in a coal mine is a key element in the game. mid-England full history of English football and record numbers no English striker could achieve after spending only two seasons in England International! Also Algerian Mahrez, who won the best in England award after being impressed with Leicester to become one of the top 10 players in the world! And the funny thing is that many famous media people in Europe and even in the Arab world, they set themselves tasks when the stadium team hit the topping in half of the season, the mission promised to shave his hair completely, or send him to a win-win situation to score the title! In addition, in a referendum on the results of the season, the official body responsible for the established award for the best player in the world receives the players in Algeria for the most votes at the expense of the largest players after stripping the car in the vote, making the best of Messi .. why not!

Mahrez, an orphan father who lost his father, was a gambler immersed in France and aspired to make his son a professional player in Europe. You know, Mehrez was shocked after the death of his father, he was fifteen years old, he felt that everything was getting more serious and life was getting short, he said, and that you should meet and progress. As a result, I didn't only need Europe, he became the seventh best player in the world. The coach himself did not believe his gospel, and you know, of course, in four centers, the first place in the international reserves in the Champions League, in which the strongest teams from the strongest European leagues participate, and until the end of the season he had to score for several weeks, then at the top of the tournament the table, but it didn't improve the tournament after he asked one of the journalists from the team coach Claudio Ranieri about finishing the season in first place, but he interrupted him, exclaiming with a laugh: "it doesn't matter, we are in the Champions League, Dude, we are in the Champions League Champions League! Most important in this story is the announcement of Mayor Leicester Peter to use his intentions to name the streets of the city after the names of the team's players to sign that they value their most important media in the country because of the title they have achieved in the football tournament ...

Leicester has been extinguished now and, like previous tours at the bottom of the league standings, so he was fired by the coach, board maker due to the team's poor performance in the season of the pros, but the gospel itself is still burning and will never be extinguished because it contains many values that exceed the needs of the game and cannot be enclosed in a Leather ball passing through the grass, values are lacking and we need them in our daily life, success and health, especially a sincere act, called from the bottom of his heart, this is what he learned in football for someone who plays with his heart, not his foot. You have to fight for your dream, you will have to sacrifice and work hard for it .. Personally, I

am honored someday to tell my grandchildren that I continued
Leicester City matches in a timely and direct manner that season.

Push your opponent forward and surpass him
Since Borussia Dortmund was the team for about 13 years, the
German equivalent of financial problems threatened to sink to the
bottom, where it was necessary to pay off some debt and the
amount of money that was not in the club's treasury and was on its
way to landing, the Munich rival said " Bayern, "the building area
that saved him from bankruptcy even demanded to surpass the
crisis and fight for access to the Bundesliga, although he was one of
the strongest contenders. This is football, you pay your enemies and
overtake them deservedly, at least enjoy this game as well as high
integrity, competitive spirit and values embedded in the reflection
of our daily life.

Complete and real
Since more than 10 years the team faced the Barcelona of the
Spanish financial management crisis, and there was only skipper
Carlos Puyol, like his team-mate Xavi Hernandez, to forgo some of
his money contributions for the club, so hide your debts and
contribute in the solution to the crisis .. remember that many big
players or unsung ones they make this magnificent gesture with
their teams and do not allow much of this news, the bright side
shows that the game of football is not limited to water. Also, don't
forget about the philanthropy arising from football matches with
the participation of top stars.

Opinions of specialists and members of the Council
"Playing with your foot is one thing, but playing with his heart is
quite another." (Cristiano Ronaldo)

Football is not just a fee and training plans for a coach's tactical
leadership, being a successful coach does not mean being aware of
the knowledge of the steps and tactical world of football, but being

able to communicate with your players and communicate your messages to them in such a way that they move with their emotions, this is an excuse for the greatest coaches and their ways in history, an enchanting round against the Argentinean Diego Simeone, who ran the team (Atlético Madrid) with several individual skills and was teeming with stars like senior rivals to compete and sweat and rejoice that it requires of them. Like the able old Italian Claudio Ranieri to win a big fan of the small. This proves that this war is not about perceiving the size of the game and putting cars to compete for victory, planting cars are the players who are in the stadium as a body only when they are present in a potential physical or physical and do not see the destination from registering goals for fame and money, and as long as the success in football exceeds the size of the game, they are, in my opinion, more than just a game, it is much deeper.

The dark side of football
It is true that football is a beautiful game and a lot of dimensional value, but when it turns to action and violation of humanity, they go beyond and get to the source of intimidation and corruption of the real, can even go as far as the death of people, as happened in many sporting events which led to overthinking and turn into real disasters. I am not talking about injuries or incidents that regularly occur as a result of the events of football, but I will mention some incidents that have remained in the minds of every atrocity that shook the world by their weirdness and their causes, but brought together by one common denominator, namely, the irritants of this ferocious game.

Killed my own target!
The news may seem a little strange and unacceptable, but it is real once I have remained conscious from the moment it appeared until today. That was 23 years ago the murder of a Colombian player who was shot over a goal scored by mistake in his team's crosshair. Colombia was then a poor country, but it had the honor

of participating in the World Cup, content with the tail of a potential bull. Colombia's 1994 World Cup regular income among title contenders was wagered that it would greatly outperform most forecasters - it is the personality of the hero, so the Colombian Mafia organizations were one of the bookmakers to win their World Cup, confident in their capabilities stars. It was a surprise that Colombia left the first round after falling in the first group along with Romania, America and Switzerland, Colombia staggered in its first loss to Romania, so we must avoid losing the next game that will unite them with the corresponding USA, and this is where the problems began, because the affected players of the Colombian threats are seriously worried to the point that some of the Colombian players have refused to play. Colombia has entered the match ahead of the United States with all its might since the referee's whistle went off, but it fell and lost the match with the intent to humiliate and after a cross-pass by important American John Hara, was reflected in a product photo for their Colombian defender Andres Escobar to call them his own nets by error instead of sending the bail out mid-world championship, Escobar fell to the ground after a move goal before I finish the game, but the value of this gift is expensive, where he sent the product of the official tournament, thus ending the dreams of the golden generation Colombian World Cup after of how he was a strong candidate for a bride.

After five days of the match and on the night of July 2, 1996, it was Colombian defender Andres Escobar who left the Medellin nightclub at half past eight in the morning, the Colombian was heading to his own car after he parted with his friends who were in the process of the evening with them and three suspicious men suddenly appeared in his car, said they were drunk, they talked a lot with Escobar, and then both of them fired 12 bullets and then ran away, leaving Escobar to bleed to death before being transported to the hospital in an attempt to save him, but he died less than an hour later.

The achievement of this incident with a major big shock shook Colombia as a whole and how a global event spread with lightning speed and spread with speculation and speculation. And in the statements of the Colombian national team coach Francisco Maturana about firearms, which were reported to the Colombian mission, which continued to face death threats in the United States if Colombia left the World Cup, it was emphasized that the threat was strong, direct and did not need more and in fact turned out to be serious a threat such as the killing of villains in Colombia, most notably the pro's view that the goal of equals in Colombia's withdrawal from the World Cup was the root cause of the crime. Since some thought that the reason to kill Escobar was better than the big drug dealers to beat Colombia at the World Cup, as Escobar makes the greatest contribution to say goodbye to the tournament from the first round and spend his profits on them, they were filtered. In addition, according to some reports, it was two days after the incident that the Colombian police arrested two murderers, who confessed that they were drunk when they shot at the defender, 27-year-old Navia, intentionally killing him.

Was the funeral in the presence of a massive crowd of more than one hundred and twenty thousand mourners, led by the President of the Republic and bringing each of them an image of memories and Escobar to preserve his memory, to prevent the Colombian union from wearing the number he wore on his team, his thanks to player.

The traces of this incident are causing outrage in sports circles and the International Football Federation is mourning the death of the player it was a crime I speak in memory of the 1994 World Cup, which ended with the coronation of Brazil. The reason for the murder of the player by the Colombian is still unknown, but it is likely that the cause of the murder was the Yakuza, the Colombian and at the same time some see that the spherical landing of the council is the reason for this crime. Subsequently, the design of the statue of the late Escobar was developed in July 2002 to keep this anniversary of the football crisis in the minds of generations to come.

Many people have already forgotten about the murder of Escobar with the products of the criminal, who killed him in response, angry because he deprived the bookmakers of profits, but most of the evidence indicates that Andres Escobar paid with his life for a mistake in the match, you will not know too much about it, but is it reasonable defensive movement wrong in the game can lead to the death of a person? No, but apparently it is possible in football.

A canceled target that destroyed hundreds of lives
Returns the date of this incident to 1964, when it came to the enmity between the two beer states to Argentina, then, sir, despite the division of the two states on political grounds, there were other, calmer, but enmity between the two peoples and the demand for football. lost their sharpness, so that directly in the framework of the design of the South American Olympic Games Tokyo in the summer of 1964 between the elite The meeting, which took place on the international playing field in the Peruvian capital Lima in a match decisive for the determination of the interpreters of the Tokyo Olympics, the goal of progress was the share of the Argentinean national team stress at the concert stadium and the Peruvian audience. It was the first goal as a ticking time bomb detonated by the government before 6 minutes before the end of the match a non-target true for the Peruvian national team, the re-vibration of the Argentine hope grid for Peruvian fans was canceled by the government as a signal from the army commander ordering his soldiers leave the battlefield, where they blew up the stands containing more than 53 thousand participants, entered the masses of Peruvian angry hysterics and jumped from the stands to invade the battlefield. A similar attack by a helicopter gunship is an extract from a military film. The fans of the savages who filled the floor of the stadium, like monsters, raged as hard as the beholder of the stands, in order to distinguish the runner with their feet, which took

place in a hysterical manner, from some notes of the rules of the game in order to implement them, and from other movements and everything that came in front of her, from other attacking Argentines!

The scene was shocking even for the police, especially after the increased intervention and attack, and the loss of control of the situation, which caused them to shoot into the air and throw heavy gas bombs in the north to prevent the influx of more fans, but this increased the panic of the masses and their fear of it. that the fight becomes especially sharp in the stands, and the insult to injury closes the gates of the stadium, and ignorance of the elements of the company outside the doors, the war, the grinding that takes place in the stadium, but the masses of paranoids led to breaking it.

There are already many fans outside the stadium, rioting and causing damage to public and private property.

The 328 killed and 500 injured were the result of the Lima disaster, most of them died of suffocation or bleeding, and that most of the dead were from the Argentine masses, and all this was because the goal was canceled by the rule of the game, so that some Peruvians gathered then before home of President Fernando Billund, asking him to step in to intercept the 1-1 score for the match, so keep hoping for a beer to qualify. But the Argentine was calculated directly for the Olympics and fought with Brazil for second place, losing 4 goals for Brazil's trip to Tokyo and watching the Peruvians.

After the incident, the capacity of the stadium was reduced from 53,000 to 42,000 seats before I renew again. in 2004 I hug the America's Beer Cup myself. The remaining case in the minds of everyone and some is considered the worst disaster in the history of football because of the large number of deaths and harsh punishments that you decided to do with the political enmity between the two peoples and led to a massacre in every sense of the word, a massacre, the outcome of which is rare we find even in the main war and military attacks were caused by the canceling of a goal in the playoffs.

Football is a square meeting of a mini-combine of novelty and relief, subject to external influences and bonuses of seriousness, they are more than simple, it is more valuable than you think, on the eve of May 24, 1964 the greatest proof of this.

How many lives were lost because of this cruel game!
Football crimes are not limited only to stadiums or players, but also among ordinary people and to questions in the courts, where there is a Brazilian study conducted many years ago that 42 murders due to football occurred in Brazil between 2004 and 2014! How high is the name of Italy, Argentina, intolerance to spherical brutality as a result of murder, and to ensure that this information is on the search engines, you will find wonders. It won't get far, because if you look at each of you around, he will see the damage that football does in society and in everyday life.

Assassin's Creed: True Story

Could Creed (Assassin's Creed), one of the most famous and most successful games in history, have sold over one hundred million copies of the series at release, if not? The allow everyone to buy them after watching them for a promotional game released in 2006, and aims to vote on the custom to sell them to get their own version of the actress, has been the admiration of all who bought it, did you day a copy of your own?

Was creed or the doctrine of the assassinator, a third-person perspective-corrected video game, was released by Ubisoft Montreal in mid-November 2007 for the Xbox 360 and PlayStation 3, and a version was released for the PC Nintendo DS handheld in 2008.

Was creed: a true story
Made the game a great success and widespread acceptance
*Having received the game with numerous favorable reviews from
all over the world, he gave it a Japanese 37 out of 40 in the view
magazine, got a 9 out of 10 from GameSpot, as well as a full party
magazine GamePro, as he won the title of best action game on IGN
site, which is the best game PlayStation 3 from position 1 a father.*

*Have you ever wondered, dear reader: what is the reason for the
great success of this game?*

*Let me tell you ... the highlights of what has made the game's
reputation broadcast across the globe is how you play and the
characters, but the real reason the most important is the story of
the giant game that deals with real-life characters and events.
already taking place during the period of the Crusades, depicting a
significant milestone in history.*

Game history
Was there a Creed: a real story
*Desmond Miles, the protagonist of the game look back at one of
your jumper grandparents we have no one*
*Moving the game from protagonist Desmond Miles, born 1987, who
was kidnapped by Abstergo in 2012 to get AIDS and that I hate him,
to one of his maternal ancestors, he is the bird of no man's son
(Altair ibn La-Ahad), born in 1165, to find out the location of a piece
of Eden, also called the Apple of Eden.*

Was there a Creed: a real story
Your Anima Photography reads genetic memory.
*Animus: The first to appear in the first series of games was Creed,
whose device is capable of reading genetic memory, which transfers
memories from one person to another genetically by DNA (DNA)
and can only be a device aimed at reading.*

It may be that the "leak" to the person who uses AIDS, that the emergence of things from the past at the present time could only come from her registry to see her, admits the impact of AIDS, and this is what happened to Desmond Miles in the first part business loan.

Was there a Creed: a real story
Game mix and between ages
Austro Company (Abstergo): is a subsidiary of the Knights Templar, and in order to keep people who descended from the safety of the assassins when reading the memory of their generation with AIDS and until the time of their ancestral assassins to gather enough information to enable them get a piece of Eden.

Was there a Creed: a real story
Pro .. subsidiary of the Knights Templar
Knights Templars (Templars): or Knights Templars, enemies of the Assassins in the game, and who are looking for others to get a piece of Eden and use in management to stop the wars and battles that they wanted peace, but in a different way, and this is which makes the Assassin's Creed their equivalent and they end up with their control and their power.

Apple of Eden: or a piece of Eden, it is a piece created by the first civilization that came much earlier than humans, which is the first known development and technology.

The real story of the game
Was there a Creed: a real story
The image of a specialist in the right morning and drug addicts to carry out contract killings
This word comes from the word drug addicts, a label that launched a party of Europeans on a number of assassins active during the Crusades and the creation of the Hasan bin Ali bin Muhammad bin

Sabah Humairi, or Good Morning party, which was born in 1037 AD and died in 1124 year in Persia.

Origin of the sect
The circle of drug addicts is the circle of Masiaf Nazar, who call themselves "the new call", so invite them to the imamate of Nizar in terms of the religion of God and came from his descendants. After separating this community from the Fatimids at the end of the 11th century AD and setting themselves a goal to strive for, they became the main ones in Persia and in the east. It was the founding of the good morning sect that made the castle in Iran a center not to spread his call, but to strengthen the pillars of the doctrines of his state.

Military strategy
Instead of traditional strategies and delving into deadly battles and bloodshed and overthrowing thousands of killed and wounded on both sides, I chose the Assassin State to eliminate its enemies in its own way, by killing prominent figures on the battlefields of enemies, after which Good Morning established a task force consisting of most loyal members of the Ismailia cult, labeling them as "partisans".

Was there a Creed: a real story
An ancient Persian manuscript depicting the murder of one of the drug addicts Tusi system file of the Seljuk minister in Iran They were guerrillas, professionally trained, trading and equestrian, as they were willing to die to achieve their goal. They can train their tolerance in the ranks of the enemy or the tiles needed in order to find strategic spots that allow them to carry out their tasks.

The murder of drug addicts for three centuries took place mainly in public places at the sight of people and caused horror in the soul. The partisans rarely managed to work out after their murder, some even resorted to suicide in order not to fall into the hands of enemies.

Was there a Creed: a real story
There are traces of the castle in Iran .. not so much .. it was one of the days when giving the castles of the world difficulty is difficult
The addicts' approach was largely a defensive military, with castles and fortresses built on the heights of towering mountains to be a safe haven for them in the event of any invasion.

It is estimated that the group's reasons are entirely provided by the guerrillas for Good Morning is what he did by giving them the weed and that they could enter their paradise if they were good or hellish if you did not obey his orders, therefore being the ready commando evaluation of the cannabis drug is not and take it to a garden or a place so green inside the castle Good morning and - under the influence of cannabis - he is now in heaven and let him practice on the described about paradise and when they take him out of the show when strong the desire to return to it, and the only way to return is to commit murders, and therefore ... this was the reason for the leak that Europeans - "drug addicts" launched by them.

Was creed: a true story
Movie poster helping Moulins credit production in 2016
And the production of a Hollywood movie in 2016 called (Assassin's Creed) with Michael Fassbender and Marion Cotillard tells the story of one of the assassins who lived in Spain in the fifteenth century and his grandson in the current era.

I will not keep you, dear readers, this is the most important information - the headlines of the history pens, because the history of the game is longer and more complex, and increasing the explanation of me can burn the whole story .. let you try this legendary game, however, the pleasure is very great, and give try it, you know what it's like to play a game like this ..

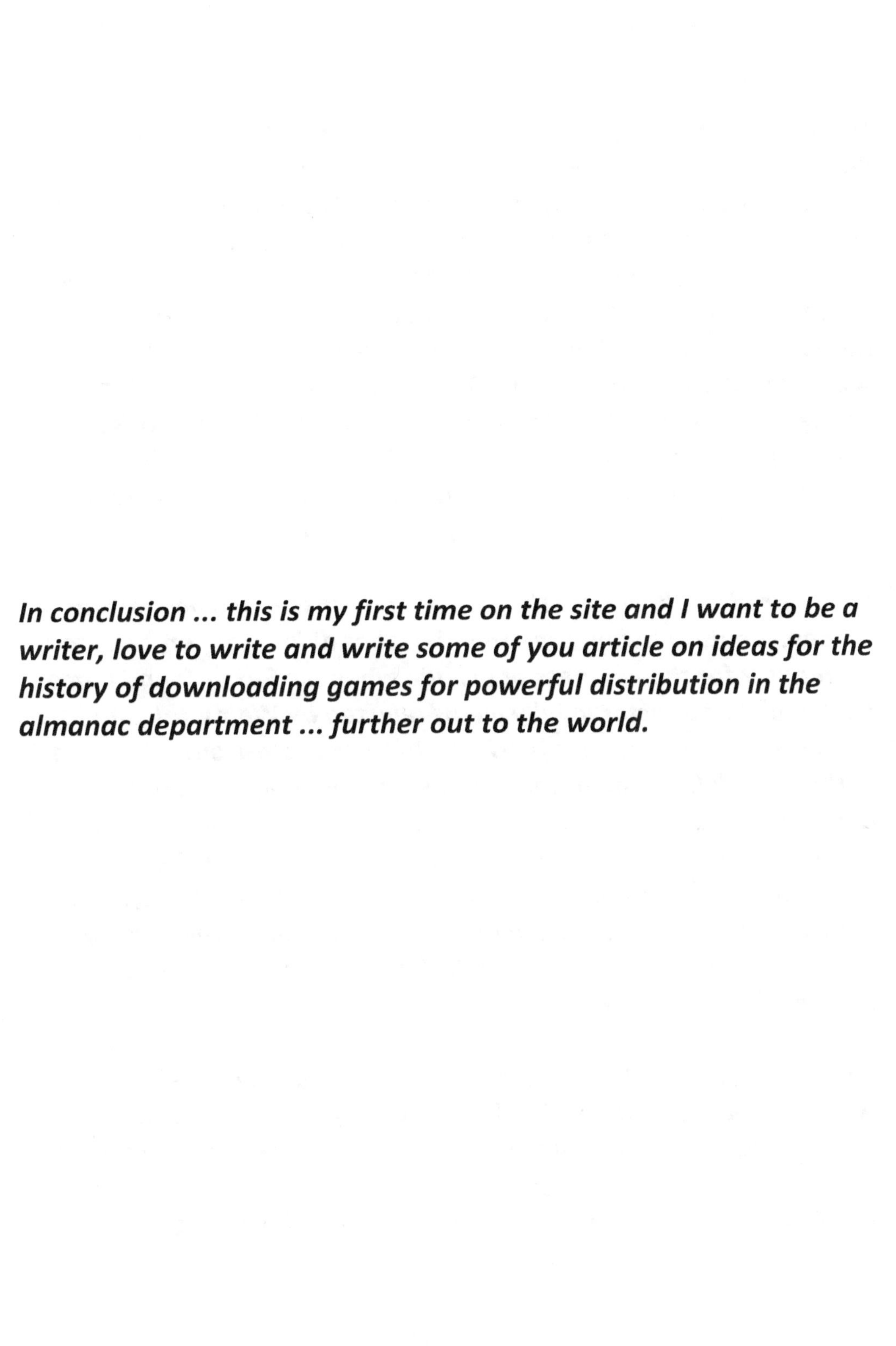

In conclusion ... this is my first time on the site and I want to be a writer, love to write and write some of you article on ideas for the history of downloading games for powerful distribution in the almanac department ... further out to the world.

You're fired

There is a famous saying: (You use every day to the fullest every day of your life can be another day). But have you ever thought that one day the worst day of your life could become or move to the beginning of the most beautiful days of your life? Yes, that's not straightforward ... many of the success stories we hear every day started with the start of the fun car, even some of the most successful celebrities today were their starting point - an accident separated them from their previous jobs, it was the best thing ever happened to them where to open them up to their ambitions is real and that as long as they want to practice it .. success stories that I have to tell them now, so from now on, let your motto always be: (yes, I I can) .. Don't despair, success never comes easily:

You're fired. Walt Disney: He dropped out of school when he was sixteen, wanting to join the army, but that didn't happen, rejected his request for the newness of his age when his father found him a job "good" as a factor in jelly yields rejected by Walt work and find a job suits him the most, practiced different professions .. they work in the ambulance, and in the restaurant, and, finally, work in animation and were kicked out of work because of their mediocrity and imagination, independent, evacuated with his brother to Hollywood and there Mickey Mouse is created, which has spread far and wide, and opened the doors of success and fame for him, and from here came the famous Friday: (Mickey Mouse is the mouse that built an empire).

Elvis Presley: Many locals tried to sign up joyfully lyric before working as a truck driver, but he was always rejected because of the ugliness of his voice, he even once sang in one of the famous theaters of Tennessee asked the owner of the Theater of Silence, because his voice is annoying, he later moved to Los Angeles and there began a journey to find who believed in his talent and it is clear what he found, from listening to him actually even became known as Elvis King.

Oprah Winfrey: lived a difficult childhood and a harsh youth, but they fought and did not give up, which ended up in the end, as the news in the station is very famous in the American state of Baltimore, but with the station master and she was fired on the grounds that her face didn't fit to appear on TV, moved to then offer a morning program in Chicago that peaked in a short period to become after a month of talk show, a program that carried his name, The Oprah Winfrey Show, and its an hour, hosted by its representatives, writers and leaders of famous people of different nationalities .. the opera is now the richest brunette woman, and her fortune is estimated at 2 billion dollars.

- You're fired. Stephen King: Before becoming one of the most important and most famous writers in the field of thrill and excitement, especially authorship of science fiction stories, his novel "Carrie" was rejected thirty times, it was said that one of the publishers was rejected her for being bored, Steve threw her in the trash can and his wife and asked them to stop it until he returned to Steve's portable and managed to bring him out to the light at the end of it.

Madonna: The singer is famous, she worked early in her life as a waitress at a donut Dunkin restaurant, was kicked out of her job after spilling drinks on a client, and I switched to submitting links to singing in bars that made their way into the world singing and glory.

Nice .. handsome .. but!

When you look at them, you feel that at first glance you are looking at an object that is perfect, perfectly flawless, then you look again and realize that it is not perfect enough! This makes you feel some satisfaction, realizing that just like you, they have their flaws, physical, but unlike the lost loved ones, these flaws have not been an inconvenience for them for many days, but if their love does not make you ignore his existence and maintain your first view of them as objects, so that completely. ...

Hilary Swank

Beautiful .. beautiful ... but!
I knew that Hillary Swank performed complex and pleasant roles precisely for her appearance in the film biography "Amelia". In addition, Richard is not, for his performance from a new fantastic role in a film biography, the last title of his "war book", rather than the expiration of the film, the romantic comedy "PS I love you", but was nominated for an Academy Award in the category "Best actor "and got them, although their teeth are big and wide, like a man's zipper.

(Hillary, like Matt Damon, doesn't notice? It's enough to get a haircut to become a man) .. this is what she said about her comedian Wanda Sykes and the Wanda Sykes Shaw charming program in 2010.

Julia Roberts
Beautiful .. beautiful ... but!
I imagined my whole mind when you smile and in fact, according to People magazine with the most beautiful smile in the world, received the title of the most beautiful woman in the world three times in a row, but hey .. Julia is not a woman with a full description, and not only that but she didn't think she was like that:

(I suffered a lot in high school from my friends taunting about the size of my big mouth, we tested jokes about the size of it, and in fact it is not their mind alone, there is a forum that told me: your mouth is big and it is never not good.) ... this is what she told Julia Roberts about her mouth and her smile in an interview with famous TV host Oprah Winfrey in 2008.

Kirsten dunst
Beautiful .. beautiful ... but!
Not the personality of Marie Antoinette, played in her other film, The closest to the truth of their relationship, their role in the movie "Interview with the Vampire" along with Tom Cruise and Brad Pitt

is closest, they really have some kind of fangs, reminiscent of what they portray us in the movies, for the vampire's fangs are long and prominent, Christina is a young actress who is connected and realizes the fact that she has some kind of fangs that resemble vampire fangs, and about this she said: all this time).

Amanda Bynes
Beautiful .. beautiful ... but!
Teen Amanda, who came to fame by offering a children's program on the Nicole channel, then moved into the world of acting as a naughty and funny girl, she said that her creature did not receive the title of beauty or beauty in the daytime: (it's like a prom in high school and be the prom queen, but I wasn't !, I was never everything, you lost your braces.My face was covered and he wasn't looking at me, and even now it doesn't bother me at all).

Lee Mitchell
Beautiful .. beautiful ... but!
The Representative has all the characteristics of a beautiful woman, but her nose is huge !, it is gorgeous dramatically, and she didn't think of ever going back to its size or shape until she said:

(It could change my acting career if you ask about it, I love myself the way I am and I don't want to look in the mirror when I see someone else moving my name).

Jennifer Garner
Beautiful .. beautiful ... but!
The nurse who loved her all in the role of the young widow in Catch and Release and has people of romance .. is actually characterized by having her big ears.! Nor is it really a problem I have Jennifer and you weren't thinking of embellishing the size of her ears in general.

Joaquin Phoenix

Beautiful .. beautiful ... but!
He has an apartment "visible" at the top of his upper lip that he knows nothing about. Rabbit, however, didn't think more than his job and a facelift in one day, and that didn't stop him from playing important roles in science fiction films, especially his role in Blades, which recounts aspects of the life of the Marquis de Sade.

Adriano push me
Beautiful .. beautiful ... but!
The owner of a wonderful performance in the biography of Manolete and the Oscar nominee for Best Actor is not ugly, but his nose is also long, and that was fine with him - the nose and its length.

Singer torrent
Beautiful .. beautiful ... but!
The nominee for a large number of Grammy Awards musical suffers from a skin condition that makes his face look like severe burns, especially when it comes to the cheekbones.

Owen Wilson
Beautiful .. beautiful ... but!
The comedic blonde suffers from a cripple in his nose, as his nose is large and flat ..

Moby Dick's immortal romance and true story

When we talk about the romances of the sea with breaking waves and the mysterious deep below that hide a monster that destroys ships and meets sailors, the most beautiful novel that comes to mind is Moby Dick's Moby Dick, in that novel that speaks of a captain named Ahab , about that stern man leaning on his tree after he lost his leg while fishing earlier because one of the whales bit her, so the captain decides to take a cruise aboard his ship, which bears the name of a bicycle, to catch sperm whales and benefit from the oils that are extracted from them, where the whale oil from the goods necessary, and even expensive, sent the ship on a fishing trip for a long time and the sailors hoped for the health of the bumper This will save them money and their families, but they do not know that the captain wanted revenge the white whale that caused the loss of his leg, and he called the name of Moby Dick Moby Dick, and in the middle of the sea, the Captain learns of the golden reward for the first person to see this whale and will direct him to him, and in fact finds Captain Ahab, who watches and watches as the chase with the white whale and the Whale cunningly eludes them, but the captain does not give up and continues to chase him, which leads to a tragic end for him and his sailors in the story of man's struggle with nature and the inevitable end of this conflict.

The author of Moby Dick's novel is the American novelist Herman Melville, published in 1851, but he experienced frustration and despair at the failure of the novel and ignored critics, forcing him to work in the basket of assembling you American so the last of the nineteenth century died.

And do not buy links and do not do it in 1907, when they took one of the ingredients of the famous, and later became the work of dozens of films, from this novel and from another, that business is not in the heart of the sea, but in the heart of the sea, and that is why the Americans got a film by Ron Howard starring Chris Hemsworth and Benjamin Walker and Judy Moll and other actors and was released without Kino on December 7, 2015.
And this is proof that the novel has become immortal and still produces films about her, but Herman Melville did not see this success of his novel and is liked as much as the creators who do not see the fruits of their success, which not many people know that Moby's novel Dick was inspired by Herman Melville's The Story of Time and is the accident of the sinking of the ship Essex, which he listened to in The Survivors, including Captain George Pollard and his mate Owen Chase and some of the surviving sailors.

Essex ship voyage
First, let's find out on this ship that the Essex was built in 1799 and has a length of about 27 meters and carries 5 small survival boats on board, and despite the fact that its dimensions are small compared to whaling ships- it is known that he acquired a good reputation for a successful voyage, and on August 12, 1819, the inhabitants of the island left not half of Massachusetts from America in the crew of the ship "Essex", but the twentieth, led by Captain George Pollard, a young man who did not exceed the age of thirty years, and also the rest of the sailors aged twenty and thirty.

Published the ship and began the journey and its goal is to reach the western coast of South America, where sperm whales live in that area of the Pacific Ocean, but the wind came in spite of what they buy, after two days of travel, the ship suffered a storm very close to sink it. and caused in the destruction of the sail upward and the wreck of part of the mast and the lifeboat, but this did not affect the determination of Captain Pollard, who continued the journey, despite such damage, and the ship arrived at Cape Horn (1) Five months later and that in the month of January 1820 years, and it considered the delay in the planned voyage, which left the sailors disappointed and they felt that bad luck might befall them, and after that I turned. The ship rounded Cape Horn and arrived on the west coast of South America for an interview.

Learning to Captain Pollard that the water was free of whales, and that the hunting season was over due to a belated departure, and advising some sailors and ships passing by them that they were expecting their ship in an area 4,600 kilometers from their position in the eastern parts of the Pacific Ocean, where fishing is plentiful, but the distance from the mainland and the adjacent islands in this area was abandoned due to the acceptance by the people of its cannibalistic tribes, the captain decided to go, but before that the idea of reforming the damage to the ship and boats was rejected. rescue, since their food and water supply was on the verge of strength, that the ship stopped at the island of St. Florian (2) in the Jala Backus archipelago (3) and there was a ship repair, and within seven days I could have collected about 300 turtles huge ones and they put a ship to provide them with fresh meat., these turtles do not eat much, and while wandering around the island, one of them named Thomas Shipp the island of fire for flirting with his friends, but drought and winds made the fire spread and their union and were able to save them miraculously, and as their ship sailed they saw columns of smoke rising from the island, which became sterile and died out in turtles and birds, and swore to Captain Pollard the punishment was equal to the incident, and already I think that Toms was flogged a few days later as punishment for what he had done, and finally the vessel arrived in the fishing area near Miss Island (4), and on November 16 one of the small vessels wrecked while hunting for one of the whales, because it is not about chasing and fishing, and on the morning of the 20th day of November 1820 he sailed as Owen Chase's first mate in pursuit of one whale, but the boat was damaged, forcing Chase to return to the ship in disgrace of defeat, and so far sitting on the deck, busy with this legal reform, I saw sailors, a white whale of enormous length about 26 meters.,

This whale suddenly appeared on the surface of the water and without movement, and then, without warning, began to beat the whale with aspects of the ship, and although it was Captain Bullard of the sailors did not attack the whale with spears, for fear of increasing its anger, and after several blows, the whale disappeared deep into sea and realizations the sailors breathed a sigh of relief and thought that the whale had disappeared, but that not a moment passed until they felt a vibration from under their feet, and I can Smurf that pushed the ship in two halves, then ever before for him and did not appear again.
And in the midst of the wreckage floating on the surface of the water, try Captain Pollard and his sailors to save what can be saved from food and drink, and stay with them three boats click small, and the distribution of the ship's crew of survivors was the first composition of Captain George Pollard and took the help of Owen Chase to measure the second composition, and Captain Matthew Joe headed the composition of the second, and due to the weakness of the boats and the inability to withstand strong waves, the sailors decided to tie their boats with some three pieces of wood and nails and there was very little drink between them and the food tasted extremely salty due to the moist seawater.

And a week later, food and drink ended and the passenger began to suffer from hunger and thirst, and some drank urine and rinsed water from the sea, maybe this quenched his thirst, the situation

was catastrophic and so hot, the sun reflected its rays on the pages of water and exploded their beaming faces, and after debate and controversy between them over their fear of the possibility that Henderson Island (5) is inhabited by cannibals, and with this Captain Pollard, sailing to this island, faced another option.
And when they arrived on the coast of the island, the detachment sent by the captain went to investigate it with caution, and let the detachment return and assured him that the island was deserted and there was no tribe, greeted the sailors on that island, within a week they married on the water of a small stream, they found it there, as they ate the leaves of the trees, and the eggs of the birds, and the kinds of goods they found on the beaches of the island and in the forest, but the food is already almost in force, and that the captain decided to leave the island, and but three of them decided stay on the island, and they and Seth Weeks and Thomas Chapple are downloading, the rest of the sailors swam very much with their experiences on December 27 and already Captain Pollard plans to reach the IS island (6) within three days and but cannot be disappointed He was injured on January 4, when discovered that the boat had deviated from its course and the amount of food in force began and death circled around them, and it was the first illness of the second mate Matthew Joy, and he wanted to spend the rest of his time by with Captain Pollard and died along with his boat and was buried at sea on January 10, and the next day a strong gust of Owen Chase's separate vehicle blew beside the others.

And on January 18, Matt Richard Peterson in Owen Chase's boat and was buried at home, as they did with Joey, and on February 8, he died in Chase's boat and, due to the extreme hunger that his friends decided to meet, they cut open his body and drank his blood and ate his flesh, and they continued in the torn remains of her body until there was no one to eat, and because of this their struggle for survival broke out, and they all wanted to open a photo of the mat, and after three days of food exhaustion were rescued on February 18 after the 89th day of the sinking of the ship in question, as a British ship found them wandering the country a boat, which they crippled and transported the three survivors on their way to their city.

As for Judge Pollard, their fate was terrible and disastrous, in the story of January 20, from what was left of food, died on the same day one of the sailors, and Thomas supporting Lawson, and became a delicacy for his comrade, who was almost hungry, who opened them, and on January 23, Charles Schott died, and he became another easy prey for his hungry comrades, who tore the flesh, and after him was Isaac Shepard, who died on January 27, and Samuel Reed's right to be fed the next day, to prevent their comrades from staying alive, who took pleasure in drinking their blood and eating their flesh. And the next morning, the surprised sailors in Hendrik's car disappeared, no one knew what was the reason? Maybe washed away, maybe Hendrick and his comrades decided to search separately they could find a ship to rescue them, later three skeletons were found on Ducy Island (7), believed to return here and his comrades, the situation in the boat Pollard decoder tragically lost too run out of food on February 1, so they almost die of hunger and thirst, for four people to work a draw and the choice is to kill him and devour his flesh, and when you pull a straw, a short straw comes the share of young Owen's coffin is 17 years old, I thought that Captain Pollard and Try to live a little more new life this young man is his cousin, and he promised to support his mother, but young Owen was brave and refused to come to draw and by the will of fate said: This is for me no luck, what should I do? ..

And draw some more to choose to say, the execution of Owen, and the check came from the share of young Charles Ramsey Dell, the shock was hard for both of you, like a friend to kill a friend of his childhood! And Charles had a pistol with trembling hands and he could not be portrayed towards his friend, but Owen grabbed the barrel of the pistol and his face to his chest, with courage, at that moment, two eyes closed and the sound energy rumbling high

Lester Owen died covered in blood. and the weight of hunger fell on the remaining three, they finished their flesh, hunger made them like wild beasts.

And on February 11, he died from a descending ray of sharpness of hunger and thirst and the background of his companion to him, and the days went by and they were in this case and on February 23, and while they were devouring some of the bones of what was left of the remains of the children, they were noticed by the passengers of the ship called Dolphin and several sailors came down to raise them to themselves and it was Pollard and Charles in case of their shock and delirium because you went through hunger and fear, and being under the supervision of a doctor on the ship for their suffering, which lasted 93 days Since the beginning of the war, the ship sank, and on March 5, two brothers got on the ship, who brought them to their island not where they met a friend whom they were pursuing, but his companion, who was saved.
And there they inform the authorities about their comrades who left this island and were already saved on April 5, 1821, and all three were in good condition, despite the long period and their presence on the uninhabited island.

And a few months later, eight survivors returned to sail from New York and they all made their way aboard different ships, but bad luck lost the match captain George Pollard, where they usually sail at the beginning of 1822, where the ship of two brothers sank, which became his captain at the coast of the island of Hawaii due to a strong storm and many of its crew members were saved, and this incident caused a loss of confidence in shipowners and Captain Pollard, where some considered it a bad omen, accusing others of not knowing how to command ships, after which all this retired Bullard worked before to the country, and he worked as a night watchman in the center of his note, and the 20th day of February of each year was highlighted, where people locked themselves in the *same way and depicted all day to honor his memory. His comrades who died on that voyage died as Captain George Pollard in 1870. Note: fishing trips at sea this time are very serious due to the primitiveness of those ships and the lack of communications at the time, and were exposed to a large number of ships lost at sea, and there have been many recorded cases of passenger ships becoming cannibals in order to survive. and despite the stories of the naval unit that picked up the passenger ships, only humans were the monsters when they got hungry and started eating human flesh.*

American writer Herman Melville is one of many examples that talk about the suffering of creators and ignore society and do not appreciate them only after their death, so do not despair that no one offers what you offer from the network may be talent, you already have there is a time, and it is not a time for evaluation after.

Secrets behind bars

Live in his life, and he chose his memories over the days and worked them out, but there are people who stop their lives when dawn and dusk cease to be days on the gloomy walls, behind steel bars and a network of constant control over them, they eat and drink without any sense of normal life, albeit harsh, they are prisoners of conscience, crime and injustice ..

And despite many reasons, they share the same destiny, sitting there, in ARE, they share the fact to live away from their parents and loved ones, looking at the distant horizon, so that the pulse of the soul would cling to their bodies and their eyes of lost souls know their fate nearby, they are prisoners of prisons and deals on this earth.

The difference between the concept of a concluded transaction If the goal of the show is to force the accused to confess, then the methods are not humane, or more correct: torture and murder based on a person's religious, intellectual and political affiliation, such as the genocide that occurred in Nazi camps against prisoners during World War II. or the torture methods used at Guantanamo Bay by the time of our contemporary ..

The purpose of the prison is different because its main purpose: it is the discipline of prisons and rehabilitation in order to re-integrate into society

For example, some types of prisons:

1-female prison:
I run a women's prison only under the competence of a warden, while a foreign prison can be mixed, where there is a guard in a men's prison and vice versa.

Or, worse, you can give the women in prison a birth there (in case she is locked up and pregnant.)

For example, the law in force in the United States: do not allow people from prison to see her during childbirth, but lock in shackles half an hour after giving birth! And I had such a bad past that she cannot keep her child for more than 24 hours from the moment of his birth, and we have to give it to her parents or social services for orphans so that they can be adopted later.

But it was in 2007 and specifically in the Indiana State Prison in the USA that it was decided to open a guardianship hostel to keep the child for 18 months with the mother, and the mother's clothes and everything needed for free download were provided, and the program was not customized for every pregnant prisoner, but to prevent using this opportunity, due to the limited number of places in the amber, where there is a playground for foreign children dedicated to their children

- Or in Egypt, for example: Article 31 of the Children Act 2008 ((create in every prison for women and a nursery available in the feed provided by الحاضنة, and allows you to be children in prison until the child reaches the age of four, and the parent notes that during the year the first years of the child's life will be in prison.))

Because they think: this is the best for the child's psyche, since it is considered a powerful motive to re-educate his mother in the future.

2 prison events:

This is a prison involving boys (criminals) between the ages of 7 and 18, but there are some events that you must complete your sentence in an adult prison (after they reach the age of 18) and that are vulnerable to being exploited by the big .. and I see that the solution to this problem is the establishment of Prison III, the pending juvenile prison and the adult prison, where its guests aged 18 to 18 are kept .. What do you think?

And even worse, there are children who are judged as adults like:

- (Joshua Phillips) 14 years old when he hit a neighbor's son 8 years old with a baseball bat, killing her, then hid her body under his bed.

- (Eric Smith) 13 years old when he was returning home from school, frustrated by the bullies who bullied his thick glasses, and he saw that the neighbor's son took him to the back garden 3 years ago and killed him the realization of his anger.

And these children are in addition to 8 others and they all received life sentences!

- And to prevent the repetition of this behavior of distinguished boys, television programs are quickly being developed that try to embody the reality of a prison called (prison camps), where worship, where teenagers play pranks for months inside an institution that looks like a real prison to let them know what they are with. collide in case of declination completion, and already! Line up most of them after the program and they will become normal.

3-prison for long periods:

People sentenced to life imprisonment will remain in prison, but that was not what he received (Mohammed Amr, Mr.), and with this he became the oldest prisoner in Egypt, and is called (Fahad of prisons), where the prison is 39. in the era of President Abdel Nasser, and from the era of Interim President Adli Mansur, age 83 (that is, 44 years old!) Where was the transfer through them to several prisons, but he was only accused of cultivating drugs on his land because of poverty, so he deserved this punishment long ago ?! And even worse, there are old people over 70 and they are still in Arab prisons, whose feet do not deserve pardon after I spent their youth in prisons?

4 families in prison:
It is not unusual for members of the same family to be locked up together, as is usually the case in Italy or Mexico, that the difference between families was murder or drug, but I expect several generations of the same family in prison (from grandparents even grandchildren), this happens not only in North Korea, where the punishment for trying to escape from prison or leave Korea without permission is to destroy all members of your family and allow (three generations fine), and after the application of these executions of unfair old people and children, no one dares there to break the laws!

5. Prison Soldier:
There is also a military prison for lawbreakers only, as we have issued disciplinary orders ranging from days to months.

And there is a movie, a movie called The Last Castle has the latest news on this kind of prison

I watched the movie trailer:

6-prisoners of conscience:

And there is a political prison, and the prison leadership is floundering, and the owners of free opinions of lawyers, and politicians, and journalists are free, or their punishment ranges from private prisons, or sentenced to house arrest, where a person leaves the house or uses any social networks with the public, as happened with Muhammad Naguib (the first president of Egypt after the fall of the monarchy) after the coup of Gamal Abdel Nasser in 1954.

- And the difference between him and the detainee: he does not have the right to this detention only after the trial in the presence of a lawyer, since the prisoner has the right to appeal or release on bail.

- Is the world (Nelson Mandela) one of the most famous characters who ended up in a political prison, where he spent 27 years when he was convicted of conspiracy to overthrow the government, but came out in 1990 as the first black president of South Africa and received several awards? including the 1993 Nobel Peace Prize?

7 prison celebrities:
There, several famous Arab and foreign ones tried to compete ..

Review from foreign celebrities:

Secrets behind bars.
Many celebrities went to jail .. pictured by Lindsay Lohan
1st chef Martha Stewart, when she sold her shares in the company after receiving information illegally and was sentenced to 5 months in prison and 5 months in her home with a $ 30,000 fine

2-Paris Hilton, when she was driving her car without a license, locked herself in for 23 days

And there are other prisoners imprisoned for excessive alcohol or drug use.

Or Arab celebrities who faced the decision to go to jail:

Secrets behind bars.
Saadian region artist
1st Possible Execution of Mackey, after torturing her maid, locked up for 10 years with hard labor

2- Hosni's tamer when he forged his military service and sentenced to a year in prison

3-Ahmed Ezz in case you chose to copy your children where he was sentenced to 3 years in prison with a fine and with this still Ahmad insists on denial refers to An

4-Saadian region cause of sexual abuse of a French girl

And others who caught their departmental networks, prostitution or drug possession.

8-Prison Results:
After the prison council or the perpetrator of the crime has a result either positive or negative

A. positive results for:

1-prisoner remorse: better and reintegrate it as a service to society

2-preservation of the Quran in Indonesia and Saudi Arabia gives a person who died by accident (due to a car accident, for example) or is a monetary chance of his release in case of memorizing the Quran, and therefore benefited from the period of his stay in prison

3-Prison Creations:

Secrets behind bars.
Tuf Daher made cutouts from matches.
And now you become an artist or a poet because of a prison, for example (Tawfiq Daher) Lebanese prisons who killed a person, who inflicted paralysis on him, he got out of prison artist makes model wonderful with matches

4-Addiction Treatment: This can be the reason behind the jail in transparent addiction prisons, because many modern prisons have addiction treatment clinics.

5-Education: Many states have started to apply the system of exemption from the government after receiving a high school diploma or university, and this could get out of prison educated, making it easier to access work after his release from prison.

6-learn to dance collectively: in a prison in the Philippines, they teach dance (Michael Jackson) for those in need and noticed how the prison authorities scoff at the prisoners among them, as it helped dance in the car with their surprise tantrums, they saw the dance ...

7-community service: developed countries use a short period of imprisonment spent by the convict in the service of the community: for example, the streets or participating in charitable activities or the obligation of imprisonment to attend the meetings of the correctional institution.

8-get rid of your debts: he can get out of jail after paying a fine, passed by the state, to public or private individuals, or as from some wealthy benefactors

9-getting out of prison as a task: or they will become heads of state, as happened with Nelson Mandela

10-release of a prisoner for good behavior: even before the end of his term of imprisonment, and this case is decided by the commission after its interrogation of the prisoner and a thorough examination of his case

11-amnesty public or private: maybe a nationwide event gives the president a general amnesty for a group of prisoners, or maybe goes to jail with a special pardon from the president of the state for one reason or another, as happened to (Martin Garner) who tried to smuggle heroin to Thailand, and was sentenced to 40 years in prison, bad reputation, but after 22 years of his reign tried to end his life on hunger strike, but his Muslim companion convinced him. also turn off the strike .. but weird what he got after announcing the style of his royal pardon from the king of Thailand, even though he is the ruler of a Buddhist country!

12-exemption from the law of retaliation: the killer kills in the Gulf countries, but if one of the deceased's sons is pardoned, he is subject to pardon

13. marriage: there are people who got married in prison (about a person abroad) and the director of the prison was a witness of their marriage!

B. negative results for:

Secrets behind bars.
Prison is often a place of violence, more drugs and weirdness
1-back: after he was released (end of sentence) for committing another person's crime

2 - addiction: going to jail can be the reason for addiction, because there are prisons that do not allow drugs in the hostel, prisoners, and it is enough for this to be where a corrupt police officer is

3.trauma serious or permanent deterioration: can cause fights that occur between the need for many injuries and permanent deformities, where prisoners can, with force, turn toothbrushes or whatever they find like a sharp tool to protect themselves or impose their will others

4-attacks and anomalies: and this may be due to age differences and power inequalities between prisoners, but some prisoners (weak infrastructure) accept him voluntarily for the purpose of belonging to one of the prison gangs and protecting him from a rival gang or to obtain drugs or some of the benefits the leader might give him because of his relationship with one of the actor's guards

5-fight and murder: that injustice and inequality of treatment between prisons and the owner of influence and a new prison usually leads to a fight or even murder of this weak (like the Holocaust) in order to impose on the prison the power of his dominance over the rest of the prisoners.

6-Prison is weird: I am the worst that could be considered advice is to prostrate himself in front of other countries so that he is only a foreigner in this prison, because he knows that in addition to the severity of the prison, torture another himself. because after his parents and his ignorance of the language around him from a necessity that makes him constantly worry, which is why most drug smugglers who end up in a foreign country are one of two things: either jailbreak or attempted suicide!

7 - Seg:

The first solitary confinement in the world was the East Philadelphia Prison in 1829, and America alone has more than 80,000 inmates.

But please note that most of the more than prisoners experience solitary confinement have become more angry over time or their attempts to commit suicide or an injured or schizophrenic person have intensified and many of them after being released into the community cannot deal with those around them and most of them return to prison after several months of his release, that most prisons in the world do not use this method, except as a temporary punishment

8-composition of the dangerous gang in the prison:

Secrets behind bars.
There are many gangs in prisons
And here is the most dangerous thing in a foreign prison:

- Mexican mafia (or in) in an American prison, and is competent in drugs and weapons

- Aryan Brotherhood gang: and they are from white prisoners against the power of black people in US prisons, the crime is their main drug

- Familia Nostra: its members, Latin American journalists convicted of serious crimes, are a gang against a gang, Mexican

And, therefore, he will try to get the rest of the prisoners to join the gang inside the prison in order to support himself.

9-strike of customs officials over food:
May beats prison food for the purpose of suicide, but I could get it to pressure the prison administration to get some of the prisoners'

requests, as happened in February 2012, when nearly 1,800 Palestinian prisoners went on a massive hunger strike in Israeli prisons.

On May 14, an agreement was reached with the Israeli authorities to reduce the term of the arrest. administrative up to 6 months only, and allowing more family visits, and re-detaining incommunicado in the cell is normal, as before the improvement of conditions in the prison, it looks like the passive resistance of the prisoners has led in the end to a positive result!

10-coup collective:
Secrets behind bars.
Prison uprising in Brazil, where 56 people were killed and heads off It is a rebellious group and an organization of people in need of help .. just like in the prison (career) of Brazil, which became the scene of violent unrest in 1992, 111 prisoners were killed, they were shot by the police

And the reason for their riot was the overcrowding of the prison and repeated torture by the guards, as well as the lack of funds allocated for health care.

- And you got another prison mutiny (Pirates), Northern Brazil over the influence of participation between the two factions, resulted in 9 killed, and by the end of it 70 jailers were edited, the prisoners were taken hostage by them so that they put pressure on the prison authorities to fulfill their demands

11.the individual tries to escape:
There is not a single prisoner who has not come up with a way out after several days of his imprisonment, but most of them hesitate to do so for fear of punishment in case he is caught, but there are several successful attempts to escape from prisons around the world.

But please note that the fugitive is lucky to stay there for one month, because most fugitives are captured after a few days or even a few hours of escaping, and that due to the increase in surveillance cameras on the streets, as a fully prepared company is faced with such kind of emergency.

12.Mass escape of prisoners:
The biggest prisoner escape was from the 1943 loft camp, where a pit of 600 beds 3 dug 9 meters deep underground to get out of this camp by algebra, and it took them a full year to complete the ventilation of the tunnels and walls of the 90 beds, 52 tables, 34 seats and countless spoons and 1400 milk dryers, and was intended to smuggle 200 people from the camp, but the collapse of one of the tunnels made 76 prisoners can only escape from there .. in the end, they lived 73 years, and then decided to execute 50 of them ... and the survivors felt that the end result wasn't worth all the effort ... and later turned their struggle into a movie.

- Or escape the bulk of the prisoners: to the prison (Natron Valley) between Cairo and Alexandria, and on the second day of the revolution, January 25, 2011, when the attackers used armored cars to demolish the prison walls and freed 17 thousand prisoners! And later, a thousand of them were transplanted into prison, but not all.

- Watch this video about the most beautiful 10 movie jailbreak movies and some will be convinced of this fact

Knowing that there are ways to legally escape from jail incarceration, including:

- That igniting jail knitting in Brazil reduces the day of his sentence by every 3 days

- And in India, if prison yoga lowers the 15th day of every month of imprisonment, because they learn self-restraint and mitigation of spells and their anger

- And in Brazil too: the prison book for 12 reports (no summary) is well written and the mistakes of a group of books on literature and psychology and philosophy will create 24 days of his sentence and it will encourage the prisoners to read

In addition, some prisons cut their prison sentences after counting the hours spent cleaning the prison.

- Save the Quran was also adopted at the Hamas prison in the Gaza Strip, where the penalty for a full year in case of rescuing a prisoner is 5 parts, in order to discipline the soul

- Is the US health exemption for every prisoner over 65 or after 10 years or 75% of his sentence is added, because their medical care is going to be the public treasury

- Every working day of Russian prisoners was spent on the construction of railways in Siberia, and areas of the devastated state freed them from two prisons, which led to the construction of compounds in the forests of Siberia and dense at the lowest cost to the state treasury.

- Was supposed to join the US Army with the outbreak of the Vietnam War, the 5-year prison sentence is being reduced, and officials say this performance continues to this day with a difference in appointment

- Fights: In a prison (Bangkok Hilton) in Thailand, they train to tell prisoners about Thai boxing, and then arrange fights between the prisoners and allow (prison fight) and the winner of them hides behind bars.

13-death: as one of the worst negative outcomes for
And it can modify the methods of killing convicts, both deservedly
punished and those killed unjustly

Lost the use of the guillotine and this thing, and the sword, and
steel, and stoning, like the use of the electric chair and the firing
squad, and gas, and lethal injection.

- And, probably, being sentenced to death is the only person who
knows where, how and when he will definitely die!

B-people were put to death unfairly:

There are many people who have been unjustly executed all over
the world, and we mention here two cases that shocked public
opinion abroad:

Secrets behind bars.
George Steny Child was electrocuted.
1 - black boy (George Steney) is the youngest person to die in the
electric chair and was then 14 years old after being charged with
the murder of two children based on the testimony of one witness
who saw them with him before the bodies were found, and after 70
years of his execution his innocence appeared 2004

2 - (Timothy Evans) was arrested in 1950 for the murder of his wife
and his child despite (Christie's) neighbor doing it, but his stuttering
and anxiety during the investigation led eventually to his execution
by hanging just through 3 days of arrest! And later they arrested a
neighbor and I think that he is a serial killer and he killed Timothy's
wife and his daughter, and this case became the reason for Britain's
abolition of the death penalty from her law

14 people were sentenced to fictitious sentences:

But there the results are lost for some time, I got caught by some criminals in the position of judicial illogicality! Like :

1 - (Osman Kenawi and the beautiful Zug) and sentenced to ((43,000 years)) two events in Madrid in 2004 and killed 192 people

2nd (Shmoe Tapies) from Thailand, was sentenced ((141078)) to imprisonment for 16 thousand people, for 200 million dollars

15 - people unfairly imprisoned:
And the opinion that the worst results in prison are when you worship a person unfairly, as happened with:

Secrets behind bars.
The judge also considered the diplomatic users of Kwame Eje after I proved that he was convicted and imprisoned for 40 years unfairly - (Users of Kwame Aha) while locked up at the age of 17 - and got out at the age of 57 after 40 years in prison when a convict killed him unjustly for the world conflict in Cleveland .. and he cries when I know the judge about his innocence that forced her down from the podium to the Senate, all because the main witness in the case withdrew his testimony after all these years ... and got (Kwame) $ 4.1 million in compensation or lost a student judge, which fixes the criminal justice system who was the reason for his imprisonment unfairly

And prisons all over the world are full of people like Kwame who are still waiting for justice and their right!

Notes:
1.There are new solutions to alleviate prison problems:

In New York Prison, like they did, 3 new measures mitigated many of the prison's problems:

Secrets behind bars.
Department of Plain X-ray of the Brain
1-panoramic x-ray of the chair: does the chair rail look like an inspection email for airport bags, so they can easily find a weapon, an artifact hidden by prisoners inside their clothes or even between their body parts

2- feeding the blind: some inmates work in the prison kitchen to ease their sentences, but problems can arise when they put some food on a prisoner who hates him, and also the New York City prison has put a wall between the cook and the prison so they can't see only the hands of the prisoners, and this speaks of a fight at dinner.

3.the inspection is sudden: that the company's management back inspection tours and the violence was sharp and once the mg led to the discovery of a large number of weapons and drugs, where I did not have time to hide them to the prisoner

2 prisons tend to have wellbeing:

Secrets behind bars.
Chambers-like hotel rooms in the prison range Spanish
1-like: prison (range) of Spain, and dedicated to more prisoners who have small children, who have spacious rooms with lots of toys, so that the prisoner's family can share his room for days or even weeks!

2. Prison (San Antonio) Venezuela: He also called the prison a party for women inmates, and is a nightclub with a pool and barbecue, allowing family and friends to enter, and supplying the prison administration with marijuana for female prisoners!

3. prison (sample) Finland and there is a small house above a secluded island where criminals live, since the neighbors are both unlocked at home, and they talk together, reconstruct the island and live together like a big family

3-prisons turned into hotels:

Secrets behind bars.
The Liberty Hotel in Boston was a prison.
Remember how the prison (crisis) of the Dutch, who were imprisoned for a year and a half, and then they rebuilt it, and opened its doors to tourists as a luxury hotel, and there were veteran prisoners among the hotel guests, to whom they gave their memories between the walls of the prison , their old friends.

4.An abandoned prison:

The end of prisons: either to leave and threaten or talk about the benefits, tourists also ended up in the jail (Alcatraz) and the Rock Stadium and this is a federal prison built on an island in the San Francisco Bay Area, United States of America and this prison was closed in 1963 and was reformed later to find out the policy.

And he made several films about the attempts of prisoners to escape from this terrible prison, where the control is as cruel as the prohibitions of nature, such as the height of the skyscrapers and the flow of its water, dangerous shark-infested

Shula Cohen, "The Pearl of the Mossad"

It was rumored that she succeeded in carrying out the decision of the Year of Lebanese most famous politicians and government officials thanks to her thin female slag smelting of hatred towards them, even became completely spies for Jews in general for months and won several titles and awards, including:

- Name pia mater

- Title James Bond Israel

Is that Shula Cohen ?!
Chul ko, "The Pearl of the Mossad."

Born in Argentina and married a tradeswoman, Jewish woman, Lebanese

Her full name Home Meyer Cohen was born in Argentina in 1917 in 1920, then her family rose to Iraq to coordinate actions between Bakuba and Basra, and then to Palestine to arrive in Haifa to settle on their day since 1937. But Schulte returned to Beirut after she married the Jewish Lebanese Joseph Kishu, owner of a shop in the photo theft market in downtown Beirut, and began her job as a Mossad agent in 1947 .. And of course it was not Scholes or some then another woman who believes in the Jews' dream of the State of Israel or the promised Jerusalem, so I decided to give my services free of charge to the Zionists, using for this purpose the peculiarity of an irresistible poison, it seems to be heavenly in the taste of most politicians, without establishing the slightest respect for the harsh consequences. not sexual services and body language, there are services that hundreds of high-ranking officials of the state between 1947 and 1961, often received clients in their home in the antique ghetto of Beirut called Wadi Abu Jamil.

It was the is stock support machine that hacked in force the key institutions of Lebanon, facilitated the transfer of information, reports and files on economic, military and political issues from the most important states of the region, such as Lebanon, Syria, Iraq and Palestine. He is equipped by the Mossad with all the necessary listening devices and records and reports, especially after he expanded his sexual activities and in 1956 five brothels occupied his beauties and the glamorous prostitutes of local and foreign women were the most beautiful. at all. a girl named "Lucy Copley" is four to ten springs and is imprisoned by senior officials without the other. This has been portrayed by many politicians and military officials who make decisions at meetings of the Reds with goals, since they do not expect that in the bosom of a warm can of dignity there will be those two to please their bodies and theirs.

Chul ko, "The Pearl of the Mossad."

Beirut in the fifties
The hired after the restaurant turned it into a bar called "Rambo Dor" in Red Beirut, where his recruits to transport parts for the Zionists succeeded in ousting thousands of Arab Jews from Lebanon, Syria, Iraq and smuggling fortune money, where a Jewish officer helped " Edward Hess "used on the way to bankruptcy, fled from the beginning of the next Jewish Lebanese" mail now "in millions of pounds, which he stole from banks, trade, then it was the smuggling of the next" Abraham Mizrahi ", the next famous Trabelsi to Greece and then his fiancée, "Lili Mizrachi", remained in the occupied territories, and in Lebanon she helped Schultz smuggle even more.

End of activity
Chul ko, "The Pearl of the Mossad."
James Bond Israel .. I fell into the clutches of the Lebanese authorities
Continuing with Shulu Cohen for fourteen years, select the most important institutions sensitive to Lebanon to allow the colonel of the Lebanese "road of the newest" effect of the Lebanese security and intelligence process, led by Lebanese officer George Barakat, to stop adapting and using husband Joseph, after becoming involved after months of controlled trafficking in apartments adjacent to her apartment, I think a number of their partners on July 9, 1962.

Court
At the trial, Scholl admitted that she was recruited as an agent of the Mossad, also admitted her involvement in the transport of dangerous and delicate files, sentenced to death, sentenced to twenty years, and then released her in 1967 after only five years of captivity. in exchange for prisoners after the Six Day War against three officers who fled from Syria according to the number of Arab prisoners.

Her death

Chul ko, "The Pearl of the Mossad."
She lived to be a hundred
The dead come to life on May 22, 2017 in a hospital in occupied Jerusalem at about the age of a boat horn.

She told her son "Isaac in Art" (he was Israel's ambassador to Egypt from 2009 to 2011): "My mother was bright, even the thoughts of her last moments are incredible."

Thus, the folded page, the most dangerous spy in the Middle East.

Cinema
Let us remind you that the Lebanese director "Fuad Quri" shot a film called "Shola Cohen, Pearl", where our story about the most prominent stations of her life, noted the role of Cheol, the representative of the Lebanese "Daren Hamza".

Fire ants ... an army chasing countries

What's on your mind? dear reader, while the ants are small ?!

Basically, you will immediately conjure up a black ant, known and widespread at the world level, that the depository object in its behavior is comparable to other species of ants, which are estimated at about 12,000 species, but in this article you will learn about one of the most ferocious and strongest species of ants and active struggle, which is known as "fire ants" or "red people".

Fire ants
Fire ants .. a generation that spent bed states
There are several types ... and so are my hands. for red
Fire ants are named in several ant species belonging to the genus "Solenopsis", and for ant species, up to the huge ones mentioned above, it represents a gender minority for it, it has more than 200 species only.

The reason is the tolerance for pain caused by the bites of this ant species, which is comparable in strength to the pain from the effects of human bites, which can be fatal for people with allergies.

The fire ants feature a reddish-brown color — or copper — and several common names such as ant activity, tropical red ant, Red ants.

Fire ants .. a generation that spent bed states
Named for the fire because of their painful sting
They exchange fire ants for small plants and seeds, these are usually some kind of small animals, and it is difficult for them to finish them off in order to provide themselves satisfying food, and

fire ants harm the bees more than insects, so if he finds the last hive to kill him and all its contents.

Builds fire ants help him inside the soil, often build near wet areas, keep rivers and beaches, usually those of the dwellings are visible due to their presence under stones or logs or others, and in the case of using ants on fire, to find some incomprehensible a dwelling, this structure of an earthen heap is similar, therefore, a dwelling that can reach a height of 40 centimeters, and can extend further to reach the limits of a meter, the perimeter of the carousel is not less than a meter and a half, and fire ants provide a supply line of up to 6 miles!

I don't prefer fire ants, the area or its resources to other ant species, and if that happened, the war would end immediately!

Fire ants .. the generation that spent millions of dollars
Attacking insects and animals miss him very much
Can the fire ant cope with extreme climatic conditions, it is able to live in areas with high temperatures, nor is it a so-called "overwintering", but the lost one struggles in the harshest cold temperatures, despite losing 80-90% of the colony due to the cooperation of winters that we have, according to monitoring in the state of Tennessee (isn't it already fighting ?!).

Fire Ant Colony Members

Consist of a colony of fire ants of several categories, including:

Fire ants .. a generation that spent bed states
Ants consist of several categories, each of which has a specific task
- Queen: She is the only member that can navigate it, and is produced daily to look up to 1600 eggs, and is considered the queen of the largest members of the colony's size, and can live up to about seven years.

Have a file that never mates wings like males, but you grab it after mating has taken place.

- Male: The mission of gold is required to fertilize the Queen, and if they mate, until the male dies after a short period.

- Soldiers: A soldier unfastens his strong and large zipper, and his lies in defense of the colony.

- Working women: sterile females responsible for the important care of eggs and juvenile ants, as well as housing costs, food for colony members.

Fire ants are attacking me.
Since most of the ant species belonging to the genus "Solenopsis" are no longer a source of inconvenience to humans or to attack the site, it was decided to classify one of the species belonging to this sex as "Solenopsis Invicta", this kind of attack of nature, I think , the intrusion sweep, known in the United States as "imported red fire ants," and the reason for the word "imported" on the label is that the United States did not know the type of ant until a single delivery to them, which cites many different kinds of goods other than for the fire ants to attack me!

Fire ants .. a generation that spent bed states
Many people will learn about his ability
Live fire ants attack the south of the United States in general, but it is concentrated in the southeastern regions specifically, there are several other states suffering from fire ants attack on me, such as China, Taiwan and Australia.

The Food and Drug Administration of America's ability to spend more than $ 5 million annually on medical treatment, damage repairs, and cars in contaminated areas for a fire attack ... trigger a fire ant attack I spend about $ 750 million annually to repair damage to rural farm, as well as compensation for veterinarians, in addition to compensation for losses resulting from the death of animals, crop failures.

Fire ants .. a generation that spent bed states
Home or nest of fire ants
Among the 40 million Americans living in fire attack areas in the southeastern United States, about 60% of them cough every year.

Established by America a number of states affected by fire ants attacks, my national programs aimed at combating this type of ants or eliminated, but this was not mentioned, unlike Australia, which succeeded in getting rid of heavy fire attacks in their areas, however, it was not completely eliminated, and still exists.

Sworn enemy for firearms
Fire ants .. a generation that spent bed states
A red ant will meet a different species of ant.
Although the power of the fire ants perch allows it to attack and destroy animals, there is another ant species that should not be underestimated, but which includes a type of real threat to fire ants, namely the "crazy ant".

This species ends in the genus Nine, whose reputation is "insane" because of its speed and unpredictability, as well as the distribution of this species in several states, including those areas where fire ants live, especially in the United States.

So now that the crazy ant shares the same area with the fire ants, can you predict what will happen between them ?!

The answer is simple: yes, deadly battles!

Fire ants .. a generation that spent bed states

The fly demands an ant from above
Away from the crazy ant, there are two species of the family - the
Forid fly is an aggressive parasite for firearms that he says flies
home to have one of the species lay an egg on the chest of the
firearm ant, then when you remove the maggot from the egg , and
leave the chest, heading to the head to settle even a developed
one.

During her stay at the top of the ant fireworks, feed the larva to the
muscles and nerves, which means hemolymph to the Ant's muscles,
and after about two weeks, moving the larva into a new phase,
release an enzyme that makes the ant's head separate from its
body in order to melt the membrane. connecting them, and remain
resident on the detached head for another two weeks until you
move on to the next stage.

10 dangers from space that can lead to the death of civilization

The sky of the heart of the stars on a warm summer night is a beautiful sight that bewitches the eye of the beholder. I have always wanted to dive deep into the depths of this universe to find out what it contains of galaxies diagnosed with the eye, to see beauty, and the planets reveal the secret of secrets and the stars twinkle best; and since I wanted to fly in this vast universe shared by meteorites and meteorites, it is not surprising that in this article I will focus mainly on me the wonders of the cosmos do not deny your God, dear reader, to see his glory ..

But behind these twinkling witch lights are also hidden some of the most dangerous phenomena on OUR PLANET and in our existence, and this is what we will get to him in this article: 10 more things that are terrifying with the possible cosmic destruction of civilization, as we had before.

1-asteroid
10 risks of space you might want to come to the yard
A comet or asteroid of this size could lead to the life of art
Every day, jogging is done, filling the earth with dust and stones falling from space. Luckily for us, most of these things, once you try to move them through the atmosphere, will stand guard and burn it as a containment policy. And unfortunately for the dinosaurs, it sometimes, once every several million years, flies past an asteroid the size of a small town, striking and destroying everything around.

In fact, 66 million years ago, the fall of an asteroid 10 kilometers (6 miles) in length decided to take the first pictures of the earth's surface, resulting in a hole 177 kilometers (110 miles) long, a hole that would pay more than the creature that caused chaos and threatening heart and scales fit. He destroyed this asteroid, a species that roamed the earth for over 170 million years.

10 risks of space might want to come to the yard

The extinction of the dinosaurs was due to a collision with an asteroid

While it is unlikely that an asteroid will destroy Earth, NASA scientists believe that anything that increases its length by two kilometers (1.2 miles) could have dire consequences for civilization. In fact, the number of giant asteroids that pass by name is not small, for example, state 4179 (toutatis 4179) is an asteroid 5.4 kilometers (3.4 miles) long, hovering like flies on a number of planets, including Earth: Although the probability of a collision is small, the orbit of a chaotic asteroid makes it impossible to predict its outcome. A close Earth collision is slated for 2069, so hopefully NASA, which is the processing office for coordinating planetary defense, will serve to address this risk issue.

2-burst of gamma rays
10 risks of space might want to come to the yard
Star collision creates a colossal bundle of gamma sensations
As the name suggests, gamma ray bursts are bursts of powerful gamma rays. We disagree with the origin of these rays and do not know how to tune it, but it is believed that the reason for its existence is the collision of stellar neutrons with each other or, possibly, resulting from black holes.

Energy is usually released from a star in many forms. During the collision of a star with a neutron, others try to combine the two magnets of the board. And since I'm talking about the End of the World, let me suggest that the collision of a large amount of energy released in a packet of focused gamma rays could release energy so powerful that it creates an explosion halfway through the entire universe as seen from Earth.

If what about the killer of gamma-ray bursts?

Well, it depends on how far the distance is. I can say that most of the GRBs were not harmful by the time they reached us. But scientists believe that an explosion of gamma rays that occurs every five million years could be strong enough to affect the earth, which affects the ozone layer, which acts as a shield to reflect these things and thus end life on Earth!

3-solar storm
10 risks of space might want to come to the yard
Solar eruptions showered the earth with our magnetic storms
Imagine that tomorrow you wake up and the electricity may run out, are stuck with the phone you like and download open applications, and I find that it does not work. Not only that, but there was no way to restart it either. For example, the entire network has gone downwind and may remain so for days, months, or even years before being fully repaired. It is possible that the absence of sounds means a dream on the planet, which until we heard its loud cries.

A solar storm is any eruption on the surface of the Sun. This storm usually has no impact on the Earth. But sometimes it releases enough magnetic energy to travel along the Sun's magnetic field into our region, known as coronal mass ejection (CME), which can be accompanied by the release of this energy by a series of strange events, most notably electrical storms and power outages.

10 risks of space you might want to come to the yard
If you hate the storm in 1859, this is what is going to happen now. In fact, a huge solar storm made on our planet in 1859 by those known as Storm Carrington (an area located in Manchester, England), that is, a storm of natural wonders referred to by historians and scientists as the cover of the globe sparkling flowers of compassion, attested by all people, can the population of the northern part of the Earth read a newspaper in the middle of the night to the light of this great compassion. But the impact of the storm did not stop at those picturesque lights, but also affected the work of the Telegraph network, which broke down and caused a

strong electric shock to the operator, and burned the leaves, and at other times began to work by itself, despite the power outage around it! .. Although the impact of this storm is considered low because electricity and telecommunications were not as regular as they are now, but what if there is such a storm now? The physical Patricia Reeve thinks that a storm of this magnitude will have "huge consequences" on the infrastructure of the modern day you can leave entire continents in darkness.

4-galaxy collision
10 risks of space you might want to come to the yard
My Andromeda Galaxy and the Milky Way.
Some of the things you mentioned, the arising ratio is almost guaranteed, but what I'm going to talk about here is some success in arising. "Andromeda" rushes through space at a speed of 110 kilometers per second. In about four billion years, it will collide with our special Milky Way and leave a trail of gas and dust stars in its wake.

Some face-to-face design successes will be ruined. You will drive others out of the galaxy completely. As a result, you will belong to each of the two mixtures back and forth, and then work together eventually to a supermassive black hole at the center and that is the birth of a new complete galaxy.

Of course, I don't think anyone will be around four billion years old! But this is still one of the most acute dangers of space and any collision of galaxies.

5.conversion of magnetic fields
10 risks of space might want to come to the yard
What happens if you reverse the polarity of your rodent magnet? Iron molten in the ground generates a significant magnetic field. Wales, the latter plays a vital role in saving species of living things and protecting us from the harmful rays of the sun. But all

200,000-300,000 per year, by moving the poles, reverse the Earth's magnetic field . In the sense that the magnetic N Pole is reflected to become the magnetic S Pole and so on. As it was for 800,000 years, what was another switching pole of the Earth, in see do we will it switch back one day, or grandchildren ?.

Unfortunately for us, this switch and flip does not happen immediately. In fact, this process is very slow and takes up to 10,000 years. During this time, the magnetic field moves around the planet and creates columns of small temporary magnetic fields that spread across the earth and weaken the power of the word.

This makes us vulnerable to radiation that damages DNA. If you completely pick up the magnetic field, there are some devastating consequences.

6-alien invasion.
10 risks of space you might want to come to the yard
Alien invasion of Earth may not be just science fiction
What's the current catalog of alien invasions and UFO dishes? Proof of this are spaceships in the Baltic Sea, cases of abduction of these organisms by humans and statements by former Canadian Defense Minister Paul Hellyer that there are at least four types of strange alien creatures among us.

Disputes about the existence of these objects are still going on at the same level. Regardless of our belief in the existence of aliens or not, you have to admit that the solar system and planets system is not a unique case in this vast universe, and there are millions of suns inside each galaxy, and if we know that there are up to 200 billion galaxies in the universe it seems unlikely to almost think that we are only intelligent beings, no other intelligent beings in the universe as a whole.

10 risks of space you might want to come to the yard

They can devastate us when we sell bacteria and insects
*Some of the world's leading scientists, including Stephen Hawking,
know extraterrestrial life exists. In fact, over the past five years,
there has already been a real push to create a connection between
intelligent objects.*

*But Hawking, speaking about the dangers of access to the
community of those who do not know about its intentions, said
something: "The civilization that you read in one of our letters,
maybe billions of years ago and lived much earlier than the more
powerful. You can see in us no more value than what we see in
bacteria.*

*It seems that we are nothing in front of them, have not even
reached the level of bacteria in front of the intelligence and
strength of these creatures !. So what guarantee do I have that they
do not treat us with the treatment of bacteria, so that our yard is
the end of our civilization in their hands.*

7 - solar flare
10 risks of space you might want to come to the yard
*The sun, when you turned her into a giant red ... the last stage
before she died.*
*At the center of our solar system is an exceptional small star. It is
close enough to keep the ocean from freezing, and far away so that
it does not turn into a desert ... this is the sun, without which we do
not know the meaning of life.*

*In fact, the Sun is just a red dwarf, a normal star in its key stage of
life. During this stable phase, hydrogen atoms fall together to
witness the production of helium and solar radiation that
illuminates and warms our planet.*

*Unfortunately, as with all things useful and useful, we must put an
end to this .. even everyone is good to go!. In about 4.5 billion*

years, our Sun will have a lot of hydrogen gas, so at least helium will share.

10 risks of space you might want to come to the yard
Will burn the Earth and everything in it
However, after running out of fuel, the core of the Sun shrinks, as a result of which the outer layers are pulled inward by the strongest force of attraction. To remain stable, the rise in core temperature of the company expands the outer layers.

In the end, the Sun will expand to a new stage of life, a red giant that will see the ocean, and a person will turn into ash, and, finally, swallow the Sun and the earth as well.

8-loss of the moon.
10 risks of space might want to come to the yard
What if you destroy the moon, what will the poets set after!
The moon deviates from Earth at a rate of 3.8 centimeters (1.5 inches) every year. Although it is impossible to completely escape, the question arises here: What if the moon is right in front of us?

Imagine this: suppose the asteroid instead of hitting the ground is its path and it crashed the moon, what happens after that?

Well, we all know that the Earth attracts the Moon, and it also attracts us, and it so happened that when an asteroid collides with the Moon, lunar dust will form living and gather around the Earth in circles (just like Saturn). And therefore you will earn these episodes, constantly falling to the surface of the Earth and destroying everything in its path.

10 risks of space you might want to come to the yard
This is how the Earth will look after the fall of the moon
As for the loss of lunar gravity, there will be no dire consequences for the climate and weather. Pulling the tides away from the moon

slows down the rotation of our planet. Without it, you will again become a day, 10 hours, six crops of 60 degrees earth, embracing our firm in a state of confusion.

9-meteors (shooting stars)
10 risks of space you might want to come to the yard
The fish can throw our starfish and destroy us.
"Shooting stars" usually refers to the trail of gas glowing from an escaping shooting star because it is in the atmosphere. Are shooting stars real and exist correctly?

That's right, balls of burning gas that freely fly in space exist. This happens when the speed of a star is so great that it is able to leave the galaxy and freely move through the universe at tens of thousands of kilometers per second.

This ball has tremendous energy that burns everything in its path and destroys the delicate balance of the planets passing by. Fortunately for planet Earth, only about 12 of these top-secret stars have been discovered.

Knowing that the opportunity to meet one of the stars in this vast universe that we have is small. Of course, this will not stop one of the blur stars, we decided to take a tour and walk through our solar system.

10-goodbye hydrogen
10 risks of space you might want to come to the yard
Photo of scientists to one of the distant stars
Although the universe is in its golden years, the cosmic landscape looks completely different. Just like our sun, the vast majority of stars in the universe are slowly burning through their fuel, it will eventually crumble into nothing. And not just carbon.

The biggest success would be a supernova (a star that suddenly gains brightness from a catastrophic explosion and most of its mass is extinguished), or maybe even neutron stars or black holes, but even these will evaporate or change their shape to make stars less to get the same fate.

10 risks of space might want to come to the yard
We'll talk to the ice statues.
Imagine: if hydrogen were once used, there would be no more fuel left to create new stars, the universe would remain in complete darkness. This will be a temperature of -273 ° C (-459 ° F) below the assembly, or absolute zero to be precise. Any living organism can survive under these conditions.

The boy who predicted his death

Jake was born between 1470-1472 into a poor family of more than 10 members, as if that weren't enough to be born with another mouth in that family. a boring boy for the jack! in addition, and having become acquainted with the village, the dog threw mud and beat him and insulted him, became dependent on his family, and did not help him, but his mother's heart did not correspond to her to get rid of them, leaving Jack, a poor bear, two things in his village poor.

The boy who predicted his death
Jake was born into a poor family in a distant village
But Jack enjoyed the unique location where the residents noticed his tiny village, he can predict the weather and rain and the time that will be imposed on the river and areas and who will die if a disease or epidemic of the village falls, but also I can predict the identity of the thief of the past, he was found many times by the missing people of the village, where this talent and began to pursue, they tell him, and began to give him simple tasks such as plowing a field with the old revolution creature, or removing

accumulated manure and throwing it into the field and other important bitches, but Jack was happy because it made him torment people.

One fine day, and while the jack was working in the field, a man looked at the eastern edge for a very long time in this position and suddenly began to shout: "You won, you do not know how to be stunned ... Long live the king, long live the King", and sank on my knees like I'm the king standing before him. People came to him to see what was wrong with him , he told them that a great battle had taken place between Henry VI and Richard III, and for the last time I know the defeat of Henry Tudor's VTOL by the new king. People laughed where they were unaware of the world outside their village, except what happens as contact with neighboring villages or distant ones, if they pass their imaginations on the back of their horse. The Bypass Jack was sensible this time, but most of them believed him and began to spread the expertise and inauguration of the new king. And months later, having imagined a file to implement the news available to Henry VI on the throne of England liters you know about the rise of work Henry before the long months of their arrival, and after a technical question, they knew that news of the boy Jack had returned to their king, bringing with it a wonderful story.

The king thought and ordered to bring the boy to the palace to tell him that the boy was a liar, he killed him and rid the world of them, and I was honest .. well, I have no doubt that it would be useful. This ordered his men to bring him here immediately.

The boy who predicted his death
Henry VII triumph over Richard III at the Battle of Watts
In the village of Jack, the guy began to behave strangely, he runs hysterically and knocks on every door, asking to hide him, because the king's people are following him, and he shouted: "Engdal and

he, the king's people are following me, they take me to live to the royal court, save me, you will starve to death in the mansion !!! ".

He raised the dogs with his laughter and mockery of the villagers who did not open the door, and even intensified their laughter at his words, how can a man live in a palace to starve him? What nonsense is this ... no, a bloodless and stupid boy (despite his talent) took the sword in his hands, and now he (the king) !!! This is ridiculous.

But the king's men came and really took poor Jack to his inevitable fate, and when the king heard their approaching arrival, he hid his seal to the boy, and when he entered Jack on the queen, surprised by the king's girl, dirty and tattered clothes and the smell of strong breath and on his face with signs of stupidity and stupidity, and complained in his decision to bring him, but he hid his regret about calling and decided to complete his choice and said to him:

-I heard that you can find lost items, well, he stole my seal profile and I want you to show me the thief.

Take a good look at the boy in the dossier, so that in the dossier itself, the organization began to get nervous at the sight of his penetrating look, and after a few seconds, which seemed to the king for eternity, the boy said with certainty:

"Sire, the seal was not stolen, you hid it, and I can bring it to you.

The king shook the boy to get his, so Jack and without hesitation went to the place of the seal and pulled it out into the middle of the astonished audience.

The boy who predicted his death
I heard you can find missing things

The secret of the king is this boy, next to him, although his blade does not seem that he can keep himself clean, but the king benefited greatly from this advantage, and began to use it to see which of his court spies Mendes and execution, and can use it to find out the sincerity of the prisoners and spot the spies who send them to other states, also used his talent in spotting any battles that would end up with minimal casualties, and you might be able to avoid that, and Jack was right, almost in most of his predictions, but sometimes he misses and becomes a victim, so that someone is innocent, only that the king was pleased with what he received.

Then came the ill-fated Jack's materials when the king decided to go on a long-term tour of his kingdom, but he chose not to line up Jack with him where he was, despite his usefulness for a boy with neurological seizures between a period and another, leading to conflict or dysarthria in the Qur'an, it is indecent, except for organizations not to run out to the Royal Party, which he left behind in the palace with strict instructions, not to one of the personnel or service, but to beat him or treat him and improve his treatment.

But this experience did not happen like this when he fed the palace workers who were fed up with Jack because of his seizures and repetitive nerves, and if not for their fear of their king, they decided to lock him in a room in the upper Palace, away from people, I must say that one of them brought him food, it came to the four workers of the mansion and dragged Jack so on to the highest room in the palace and power, and they closed the door and hid the key, and they agreed to bring one of them every day to give food and drink for him until the king returns.

But the workers were exhausted by their work and forgot poor Jack, and days and weeks went by, people lived in the palace to hear muffled screams and sometimes hit the level, but they thought they were ghosts or spirits of the dead who return from another world on dark nights , to look with horror in the hearts of dreams, and would never have guessed that one of them, that the sounds come from one of the docks themselves, or rather, Jack.

The boy who predicted his death
They forgot Jack in the noisiest room in the palace until he died of hunger
And on that day, these voices and screams ceased, and the joy of the people who called them silence depended on the fact that the spirits returned to their world, and I, having got to them, the spirit went to its creator.

The king returned from his long journey and asked Jack, he began to service the exchange of glances between them, wondering when was the last time they saw Jack - luck with this, and angered the king and ordered an extensive search for the thought that someone had kidnapped the boy to take advantage of it after learning his secret, and began frantically looking for the heart of the palace, loud bitch, and when the sea arrived in the room in the upper palace, and began to smell musty smells coming from them, and the closer they got, the more smell, the more they found the door locked and they broke it - and the surprise was ...

Jack's body lay on the ground with his mouth open, as if the cry froze on his lips and was alert, and the body decomposed and gave off odors, and the consequences of scratches inflicted by the poor man's nails where he tried to bury himself in the floor of the room with a rocky and wiggling blow against the bars of a narrow room , were the cause of the noise and conflict, which they called that.
, as predicted: he died of hunger in the palace.